THE GLOBAL CATASTROPHE

R.S. Pedersen

R.S. Pedersen

Copyright © 2024 R.S. Pedersen

All rights reserved

The characters and events portrayed in this book are fictitious. Any similarity to real persons, living or dead, is coincidental and not intended by the author.

No part of this book may be reproduced, or stored in a retrieval system, or transmitted in any form or by any means, electronic, mechanical, photocopying, recording, or otherwise, without express written permission of the publisher.

ISBN-13: 9781068999321
ISBN-10: 9781068999321

Cover design by: J.G. Pedersen
Library of Congress Control Number: 2018675309
Printed in the United States of America

*For Angus, you have left an indelible paw print
on my heart. I will miss you always.*

CONTENTS

1

Timothy had grown cold and stiff. The growing thud of infected hammering against the house filling the room even while Charissa, Penelope, Sophia and Atticus sat prostrate with grief. Charissa had no concept of time, no inkling of how long they had flanked Timothy's body. Her hands still pressed into his unmoving stomach, staunching blood that no longer flowed. His blood lined every crevice in her hands, soaking through the towel and drying in the creases on her knuckles.

She'd noticed that Sophia's hands were similarly stained.

Timothy's final words echoed in her mind. *Protect them.* It was a mantra that drowned out the accusations of her being a murderer and stilled the swelling grief in her heart. She could blame herself for his death. If she had moved quicker, been better, anything, then maybe he would still be alive. But he wasn't and his final wish had been for her to protect his family. Nothing mattered more than that.

She pulled her hands back and rocked back on her heels. Three faces turned to watch her. "Stay here." Her voice, thin and raspy feeling a million ways wrong, cut through the increasing pounding from outside.

Her legs were stiff and the blood on her hands cracked when she flexed. Still, she forced herself to stand, to pick up her spear and move. She went down the hall to the play room and assumed her usual position at the window.

Several infected beat against the wall below her, throwing their bodies at the house with a bone breaking abandon which would be unthinkable in a living, feeling human. Charissa opened the window and chose a target, slamming the point of her spear down and lodging it into the infected skull. They collapsed and she braced herself so the spear would wrench free.

Protect them.

The words echoed in her mind, shuddering through her as she picked another target and killed it. And another. And another.

Protect them.

It filled her, leaving her with nothing else. She worked tirelessly as more and more infected arrived, drawn to their home first by the gunshots but ultimately by the knowledge that this house contained potential victims. The pile under her window grew, forcing the new arrivals to scramble over their fallen companions. More of them circled the house, clawing and throwing themselves at different segments of the walls but the majority entered the kill zone to try and reach the target they could see. To try and get her.

The sun sank, that slow nearly imperceptible sinking that it did on overcast days. The light dimmed by degrees until suddenly shadows overtook the world. When she could no longer discern one infected from another, from their shoulder or their head, Charissa withdrew her spear. She picked up a random childrens toy, something hard, with a bit of heft, and then lobbed it out the window and across the street.

It landed with a clattering which contrasted to the pounding on the house. The infected seemed to pause for a moment and Charissa held her breath. The moment stretched on and then she noted several shadowed forms lumbering after the noise and the pounding on the house resumed although at a lessened frequency.

Her arms burned and her mind was a fog of too many emotions

and too great fatigue for her to do more after that than close the window and make her way out of the room and back down the hall to the bedroom.

The house was darker than the outdoors but Charissa's eyes did their best to keep her from bumping into things. "Pen?" She asked, at the doorway, unable to see enough inside to determine where Penelope and the children were.

A light bloomed from the corner and Charissa turned away and shielded her eyes.

"Chary?" Penelope inquired.

"Yeah."

"Oh thank goodness. Get over here you stupid woman."

As her eyes adjusted to the increased light, Charissa saw that they had covered Timothy with the blanket that had been on top of the bed, the one she remembered getting brain matter from the man who shot Timothy on. She looked closer to the source of the light, Penelope's phone flashlight, and saw Penelope sitting up in bed with Sophia and Atticus wrapped around her as though they were tumors.

Charissa grunted and shuffled out of her outer layer, shedding the protective gear she had donned so long ago and which was now splattered and stained with the blood of those she had killed, before slipping in beside her sister and niece and nephew.

Sophia, who had been asleep, burrowed further into the blankets, shifting away from the cooler body of Charissa and closer, if that was possible, to her mother's.

Charissa settled herself as comfortably as she could, soaking in the ambient warmth and steering her mind away from her dead brother in law who lay less than a meter away.

*   *   *

Physical and mental exhaustion did not seem to matter when Charissa was woken at some unholy hour long before dawn to the maelstrom of her thoughts and the thudding staccato of the infected attack.

Murderer. The thought was accompanied with the memory of her spear entering that first man's body, her finger squeezing the trigger and accepting the recoil of her gun when she shot the second man, the waves of reaction nausea.

Protect them. That came with the feel of Timothy's blood on her hands, the sight of his falling, his final breath.

She shivered despite the radiant heat of the people sleeping beside her. She wondered if they were even still sleeping, or if they too felt weighed down by the darkness and all that had happened the day before. Her thoughts ran in circles, reliving every moment, every mistake, every choice.

She was helpless, smothered under the weight of her own thoughts.

Sophia shifted beside her. Turning and grasping Charissa's arm.

Protect them. She turned toward her niece, away from the edge of the bed and where she knew Timothy lay, wrapping an arm around the little girl.

"Auntie?" Sophia murmured.

Charissa swallowed down her surprise and hummed her acknowledgement.

"Are those people coming back?" Sophia's voice was so small and soft that Charissa almost couldn't make it out.

She tensed and pulled Sophia a fraction closer. "No, they won't be coming back." She heard the steel in her voice and hoped that provided her poor, traumatized niece with some measure of comfort.

“Because you killed them?”

Charissa drew in a sharp breath and contemplated her answer. “Yes.”

“Will they become monsters?”

She shook her head, although the motion would only reach Sophia as a shifting of the pillow and blanket. “No, they won’t. They were already monsters.”

Sophia nodded and buried her head into Charissa’s chest. “Are you going to kill the monsters outside?”

She licked her lips and pulled Shopia tight, “Yes I am.” She promised.

2

Those absolute imbeciles. Greg thought to himself as he read through the final lines of a Swedish scientific report requesting living samples of Xeno-1. Honestly, the word scientific was probably too generous. If someone had written something this sloppy a year ago they would have been laughed out of the scientific community, or at least Greg hoped they would have been. But now... now it warranted him wasting his precious time entertaining it.

The hypothesis boiled down to their belief that they could communicate with the infected. That the creatures had a language of sorts and that it could be learned to allow humanity to negotiate with the virus or those that sent it. It was utter, out of touch, hokum. The infected were zombies. No one negotiated with zombies. But maybe they didn't know that in Sweden? And there was the fact that zombies were fiction and the infected were real, but that didn't change the rules. Or did it?

Greg paused to reconsider his own biases. Just because fiction writers had imposed specific rules on zombies did not necessarily translate to Xeno-1. They certainly seemed to have different goals than their fictional counterparts. And wasn't there that one Will Smith movie where he communicated with the zombies?

With that in mind he leaned forward and forced himself to reread the report with a more open mind. If what the team proposed worked, then what? If they could communicate with the infected what would their minds be like? Would it be a hive mind as their former behavior suggested or would they be individuals? Would they have to negotiate with each and every one of them, bears and birds included?

He sighed and gave up reading the report for the moment. The implications flood his mind, making him blind to the words on the screen, and preventing him from utilizing his usual rudimentary understanding of science.

Every time a report from some fringe group made it to his inbox it was like this. Some out of touch academics, with no concept of the actual everyday damage this crisis was causing, wanted access to Xeno-1 so they could prove their little pet theories. Theories which ranged from the idiotic to the absurd. Even those with real grounding in science held little merit when it came to actually stopping this crisis and would be better served waiting until a real solution had been found.

What did it matter if you could talk to it if it was still bent on killing you and subsuming your body into itself?

He couldn't help but wonder what they would do if faced with an actual infected. When it came right down to it, what would he do if faced with one?

Despite how the crisis had affected his life, he had never had an actual encounter with one of them. Certainly, he'd probably read more reports and watched more hours of footage on them than anyone else, but he knew that was different than being in their actual space. That was an experience he shuddered to even contemplate. He couldn't believe there were actually people out there asking for the experience.

* * *

"Let's get going," Treegar orders adjusting the strap on her bag and walking quickly away from where they had spent the night, terribly exposed and trusting that any local infected would have been drawn away from them by the gunshots in the compound.

She could sense Garner moving behind her but didn't bother to check if the doctors were following as well. Her clothing under her gear was still caked in mud from her tussle with Wade and his guards but she'd taken off her socks during the night to let them dry and that seemed to have mostly worked.

For about half an hour she led the group on a path that seemed to keep leading them further from Salvation and, based on the position of the sun, in a south-westerly direction.

"We need to determine where we are and which way we should be going." Garner kept his voice low and his eyes on their surroundings.

"Those shots have probably attracted infected for several clicks. I say we move in a generally south western direction and sort out the particulars once we have more distance between them and us," Treegar countered. She too kept her eyes on their surroundings, forcing her shoulders to remain loose but ready to snap into a defensive posture at a moment's notice.

"That sounds reasonable," Dr Scordato chimed in. A tiny part of Treegar was glad to hear him speak. For a moment she considered inspecting that emotion but brushed the impulse away, it was too unimportant to distract her from their surroundings.

"Alright, that sends us in that direction," Garner pointed off the path they had taken and through a small copse of trees.

Treegar sighed and readied herself for the more difficult walk through undergrowth.

"How about we keep going as we are until we pass that?" Dr Nagi suggested, "I don't think trudging through undergrowth will speed our flight."

Treegar looked to Garner and on his nod set out along a path that cut more of a middle line between the two directions, allowing them to skirt the trees but placing them along a more south westerly route than previously.

3

It saw the world more clearly than ever before. The distances between its selves painted a picture, a vastness and a finiteness which it had been unable to imagine before. It saw all that it was and all that it could be. It yearned for that future and strained toward it.

*　　*　　*

The rolling landscape created an endless expanse of nothingness. Trees and rocks served as their major landmarks but under the blanket of snow even those seemed to fade. A few hours into that day's journey it began to rain in miserable sheets. The drops were less individual collections of water and more air made liquid. It collected in Jason's visor and seeped through his layers.

The only positive aspect of their journey was that they had found further signs of civilization. Their path had intersected with a road which was clogged with scattered and abandoned vehicles. If it had been practical to take one they would have, but unfortunately roving groups of infected moved through the lines of cars in the general direction of the compound. Jason didn't know what Garner and Treegar thought about taking those things on but he certainly wasn't going to push for it, no matter how numbing and miserable the rain was.

While he watched how the soldiers managed to maintain a sense of alertness, Jason could feel his own slipping. The gray sheets of rain fogged his mind until all he wanted was a warm blanket and a nap. Even the moans of the infected failed to spike his adrenaline.

One thing about the rain, it was melting the snow. Not exactly a positive since it turned the ground underneath into a slushy mess and exposed a leak in the front of his left boot. Water wicked up his sock, quickly making each step a squelching exercise in discomfort.

"We need to stop for the night." Jaspreet whispered, or at least Jason thought it was a whisper, her voice unnaturally softened by the weather.

He looked up and noticed the failing light, his eyes had been so focused on the ground and each step he took that the growing darkness had gone completely unnoticed by his fatigue fogged mind.

Garner glanced back at the pair of them, "We won't be setting up camp tonight. We need to find a house, I don't want to be out in the open with so many of those things around."

Jason nodded and looked to Jaspreet who agreed.

Jason's foot began to feel less like part of his body and more like a wooden stump as the last of the light slipped away. The party trudged through the increasing twilight, Jason focusing solely on not tripping on the shadowed and uneven ground.

Finally, "Over there." Treegar's voice was pitched low but carried clearly through the visors and the rain.

Jason and the rest of the group turned and looked where she was pointing. In the distance the rolling horizon gave way to a distinctly house-like shape. Changing course was automatic and each member of their group seemed to move with more vigor than they had displayed in the past hours. With the increased pace they quickly covered the distance to the structure, finding it to be closer than it had first appeared and if what Jason could make out in the darkness was any indication, smaller as well.

It was almost fully dark by the time they reached it. Jason was certain they were about to be ambushed by infected. He had never felt so exposed and defenseless. His foot was rapidly becoming a problem as the moisture and the numbness crept further and further up his ankle.

"Wait here." Garner ordered Jason and Jaspreet before setting out around the building to the left while Treegar did the same to the right.

Jason and Jaspreet moved so they were standing back to back, alternating their attention on the building and the deepening darkness around them. After an indeterminable length of time, somewhere between minutes and an eternity, Jason heard movement to his right. He braced himself for an attack and waited. Then a similar noise reached his ears from behind him. He felt Jaspreet shift and hoped that she too was readying herself for an attack.

"All clear." Garner's voice carried through the darkness in front of Jason.

"All clear." Treegar echoed from behind him. Jason relaxed and lowered his spear.

"Good. Did you find a way in?" Jaspreet pitched her voice to carry in a sing-songy way.

"This way." Garner beckoned.

The darkness obscured Garner completely so Jason took a chance and began tentatively shuffling in the direction of his voice. He took his steps slowly and carefully, hoping he didn't encounter any obstacles.

"Keep coming. You're almost there." Garner encouraged. Jason peered into the darkness wondering how Garner could possibly know that since he was certain that the night was just as impenetrable to the younger man. Suddenly his boot caught on something and he went pitching forward. His hands flung out in front of him, trying to brace himself with the butt of his spear but it hit something which sent it sliding forward in the slush and mud. He face planted into the ground with a loud groan.

"What happened?" Garner was suddenly at Jason's elbow making him flinch with surprise, jolting his body and sending a ricochet of pain down his leg.

"I tripped."

"Hmm." Was Garner's only reply, though it didn't feel judgmental, "You're nearly at the door, can you make it?"

Jason felt hands reaching under his arms and did his best to push himself to his feet, emitting another loud groan when his knee shrieked with pain. He shifted his weight to the other leg and ground his teeth together. He did a little test hop and nearly fell back down at the jarring pain.

"I'll help," Garner offered wedging his shoulder under Jason's armpit and lifting most of his weight.

Together they shuffled and limped into an open door that looked like a black on black painting where the interior was even more inscrutable than the exterior. The walls provided them with reasonable shelter from the constant rain.

"Just a few more steps," Garner assured. The pair hobbled into the building, the walls and lack of rain changing the quality of his voice.

"Is there a light?" Jason ground out, eager to see anything about their surroundings and maybe, find somewhere he could sit and get off his leg.

"I have one." Jaspreet spoke from behind them. There followed a sound of shuffling. Jason glanced behind him toward the door. In the comparative darkness of the building the night outside looked almost bright, though that brightness was occluded by the silhouette of who he assumed was Treegar.

Fear niggled at the back of his mind and he hesitantly called out, "Treegar?"

There was a pause as the figure shifted, stepping inside the building. Jason felt the hair on his neck rise and he fervently wished that he could support his own weight.

Finally, "It's me."

Jason released a breath and then had to shield his eyes as the world erupted into sudden blinding brilliance. He hissed at the sudden assault.

"Oh! Sorry!" Jaspreet squeaked and then the light went suddenly away again.

"Let's try that again," Garner coached, his voice only betraying a slight amount of irritation.

"Right, get ready. 1, 2, 3." Jason kept his eyes closed and watched as the veins of his eyelids became a visible red blur. He kept his eyes closed for several moments until the earlier pain had fully receded and they felt adjusted to the new light level. He squinted and blinked rapidly, keeping his head turned away from the light source and tracing Treegar's careful progress into the building. He noticed that she had closed the door behind her.

The walls are a soft yellow with prints taped directly onto it. There was a plastic tray beside the door and a mat for wiping shoes in front of it. Above was a row of pegs with two smocks hanging from them. The walls were broken up not only by the prints but also by large windows which reflected Jason and the rest of the group back at them with their images overlaying the inky blackness of the outdoors.

Under the windows sat built in shelving, the drawers in various stages of closure. Paint appeared to have been splattered and smeared along the faces of the drawers and a variety of paint paraphernalia jutted out from them. An abundance of plant pots covered the tops of the shelves with their inhabitants in various stages of death and decomposition.

Jason tugged Garner toward the nearest drawers and with his assistance made it there with only a few leg jarring hops. Garner shoved several of the pots away and then helped Jason sit in their place. Both of his legs sighed in relief as he dangled them down.

"It's a studio." Jaspreet observed, beginning to move, taking the light with her.

Jason followed her movements and saw as she shone the light on stacks of canvases, an easel, and a comfortable looking chair that unfortunately resided at the far end of the room.

"Doesn't look like there is anywhere for us to sleep." Garner observed, "let's secure the door and set up the tent."

At that order, Treegar began wedging material in front of the door. Jason swung his bag around to his front and wiped away some of the water that hadn't been shed. He hadn't paid much attention while packing but figuring out what he had been carrying was one thing he could actually do while still sitting. He pushed more of the plant pots aside and began emptying the top of his bag onto the counter. Beneath cans and packages of food lay the familiar nylon material of the tent.

"I've got the tent." He offered, pulling a section of the bundle out the top of his bag.

Garner took the whole bag from him and set it on the floor before pulling the tent the rest of the way out. He watched as Garner, Treegar and Jaspreet efficiently unrolled and set up the tent in a matter of minutes.

Once they unzipped the tent door, bags and bed rolls were

tossed inside and Jason found himself the unfortunate center of attention again. In the minutes of hanging imobile, the muscles above his knee had seized into stone. Pain spiked from it whenever his minor shifts in balance sent the appendage below swinging.

"Let's take a look at this." Garner began, kneeling down in front of Jason's dangling boot.

"It's fine, I can…" He broke off his protests with a hiss of pain as Garner's simple action of grasping his boot to begin unlacing it sent a sharp pain lancing up his leg. Jason found his mind utterly unable to form proper sentences as each gentle movement of his leg was accompanied by white hot pain.

Slowly Garner worked Jason's boot off. "Why's your sock wet?" He asked, turning Jason's boot upside down and spilling the wet contents onto the studio floor.

Jason hissed through his teeth before forming an answer, "Leak." His brain felt like mush.

"You'd better get them off and let them dry." Jaspreet noted.

Garner nodded and began rolling them off of Jason's foot. The skin underneath was pale and wrinkled. "You're foot's really cold," he observed. Garner angled Jason's foot up slightly and furrowed his brow, "we'd better let your foot dry out too, I've never seen such a pruney foot."

Jaspreet knelt beside Garner and twisted her head to get a better look at the underside of Jason's foot, "I agree. That looks like the beginning of trench foot. Is this what's wrong?" He peered up at Jason, the low lighting enhancing the depth and darkness of her eyes.

Jason shook his head, "My knee." He ground out.

Garner nodded, released the foot and began attempting to roll up the leg of Jason's pants. He made it the the roundest part of Jason's calf before the pants refused to move any further. "I'm sorry, we are either going to have to cut your pants or go at this from the other end."

Jason looked down at the soldier blankly before realization dawned on him and reluctantly nodded. With a slow breath he readjusted so that he was no longer bracing himself with his hands. Undoing the fastening of his pants was the easy part, it got more complicated after that.

"I need a little help," he admitted.

"Lift your butt and I'll pull down." Garner offered. Jaspreet stepped in and assisted each working one side of Jason's pants past where they were pinned into place by his seat on the cabinet and down his dangling legs. The cold night air rushed in and stole what little warmth Jason had retained. Goosebumps prickled up and down his skin.

The pant legs dropped to reveal two very different looking knees. One, pale and goose pimpled, but proportional to the surrounding leg. The other looked like a grapefruit. Angry, red, swollen, it wasn't surprising that his foot was so cold, this was where all his heat had gone.

"Oh my." Jaspreet gasped.

Garner gently pressed the swollen skin forcing a hiss to escape from Jason's lips. He clamped his jaw down tighter and tried to swallow pain. His stomach rolled.

Treegar pushed past Jaspreet and Garner. "This is gonna hurt so shut up." She ordered before grabbing either side of his knee and handling it.

"Ah! Mmmm... ssss!" He clamped his jaw shut to hold in the agony while her gloved hands prodded and manipulated the area. He averted his gaze, unable to witness the source of his agony. With a wrench and a pop, the pain suddenly dropped by three degrees. The relief sent him lurching forward, pushing her hands away from the injury site.

"You'll be fine now." She said coolly, "Use your wet sock as a cold compress. It's going to be an uncomfortable night." She stepped away from him and turned.

"What did you do?" Garner asked, placing a hand in gentle restraint on her arm.

"His knee cap was dislocated. I relocated it." Jason looked at her as she simply shrugged off both her diagnosis and treatment of his injury.

"How did you know?" Jaspreet inquired, saving Jason from his more expletive riddled version of the same sentence.

"Knee caps go in the front, they don't belong on the side of your leg. Besides, I've fixed them before." With that she pulled away from Garner's outstretched hand and ducked into the tent.

Jaspreet moved back to Jason and began her own probing of the area, the action no longer eliciting the same level of pain as Treegar and Garner's had. "I don't approve of how she went about it, but it seems to have fixed the problem."

Jason shook his head, "Which of us is a medical doctor?"

Jaspreet sniffed and Garner huffed a soft chuckle. "Very well then, Doctor, treat yourself." She stood and gave him a hard, motherly look. "But if you expect to be back up and walking on that leg any time soon, you'd better control that swelling and air out your foot. Do you think you can manage that?"

Jason smiled for the first time in hours and nodded, "Yes, ma'am."

"I'll take the first watch." Garner offered, "let's get you settled."

He swept in and shouldered Jason's weight, assisting him off of the cupboard and the few steps to the tent. From there Jason managed a gingerly three limbled shuffle into the tent.

4

Each mind possessed a language and a drive of their own, great and small they bent to the will of the virus, blending to create a new language but it was in the oldest parts of itself that the virus found the deepest truths. In the depths of its memory, for a time before the first mind bent to its will lay strange knowledge. In flashes these memories would over take it, rising to the surface as melting oil in water, gathering and changing the surface of what it knew.

*   *   *

Penelope spent the night wrapped around her children with Charissa awkwardly bookending them at the edge of the bed. Tim lay where he had died, but a blanket had been draped over him and unnecessarily tucked around him by his wife and children. His final words to her, and the promise she had given pounded in her mind along with the pounding of the infected. Through the long dark hours of the night she couldn't help but conjure horrible scenarios where one got in, they all got in, or Timothy and the others rose from the dead.

When Charissa could no longer stand the uncertainty of her imaginings, she slipped out of the bed. Shifting her body so that it nearly fell off the edge and easing her arm away from where Sophia had fallen asleep clinging to it, and made her way out of the bed without obviously disturbing anyone. From there she crept out of the bedroom, fumbling for her spear which had been left leaning by the door, and made her way soft footed out the door and down the hallway. There wasn't enough ambient light to avoid the drying puddles and trails of human fluids but she did her best to avoid them by memory. Nothing soaked through the soles of her socks so she knew she was at least marginally successful.

Entering the play room, she listened to the moans and thuds of the infected until false dawn cracked and she began to be able to make out individual shapes. Once heads became discernible from shoulders, she lifted her spear, opened the window and began.

There were so many infected that they practically pushed themselves onto her spear. The pile grew and grew until new ones were unable to reach the actual side of the house under Charissa's window. Charissa stared at the face of an infected, their gender completely erased by decay, hair that might have been brown or black or blonde now hung in ragged clumps held on by dry, withered, sallow, skin. *This is the future,* she thought, *this is what we become now.*

The thought held a weight in a way that nothing in her life had before. This was her destiny. This was the destiny of all the earth. There was no escaping it. And resisting... she shuddered at the memories, resisting meant being a killer, a murderer, a monster.

She watched as that particular infected clawed and scrambled over its immobile companions, bony fingers and bare feet slipping and crushing in their drive forward. She held her spear at the ready, angled to catch their head if only they got close enough.

"So, this is where you've been," Penelope commented from the doorway.

Charissa ripped her eyes from the infected and straightened up.

"We were worried. Are you doing okay?" She moved closer. Charissa could still make out the imprint of her pillow in her face. How she had managed to sleep at all with her dead husband in the room astounded Charissa.

"I'm fine. Just focused on protecting you and the kids," She deflected. She wasn't important. She just needed to fulfill her promise.

"Ha. You're not fine. None of us are fine." Penelope slid down with her back pressed to the wall until she was sitting on the floor and let out a mirthless chuckle. "We just spent the night with my dead husband, your dead brother in law, and the kids dead dad. We are not fine. You couldn't even sleep in there could you? You're never that still and your breathing never evened out. Don't think I didn't notice. We should have moved him. That night is going to haunt my babies for the rest of their lives. I know it's going to haunt me. So, cut the crap, how are you really doing?"

Penelope stared at Charissa as though the force of her mind could unlock her sister's secrets. Even when Charissa dipped her head and looked back out the window she could feel her sister's eyes burrowing into her skull.

She drew in a small breath and submitted to the inevitable. She was too tired to fight and too tired for a false sense of emotional stability. "I'm a monster." It was all she could get out before her throat closed up.

Silence met her declaration, leaving her with a growing sense of dread until she finally turned back to risk seeing Penelope's reaction. Her eyes were wide but her brow was furrowed and her mouth set in a tight frown.

"You're not." She denied.

Charissa shook her head and turned back to the window. The infected she had been watching had gotten their foot stuck in the ribcage of an immobilized infected and was trying to drag the body toward the house with them despite the fact that it was pinned down by at least two other immobilized bodies.

"I mean it. You are no more a monster than I am. No more than any of us has to be!" Her words carried and sent the struggling infected into a frenzy. They thrashed and clawed until their own blackened blood oozed over their comrades.

"Look at me!" Penelope insisted, grasping Charissa's shoulders and forcing her to turn from the window. She had a fierce look in her eyes that Charissa knew from growing up with her, this was Penelope's righteous indignation as she embarked on a campaign to fix something she saw as wrong or unjust.

"You are not a monster. You are my sister and I love you. Sophia and Atticus love you. You did exactly what you had to do yesterday to protect them and save them from becoming more of those." She gestured out the window. "You are a good person. You defended children from people who would have harmed them. If those people would have listened to reason or shown some compassion, we wouldn't have done what we did, but they didn't and they deserved what came to them."

Charissa felt a small piece of her shame break off and shatter. She might be a killer but she wasn't a monster. It wasn't much but it was something. The change must have registered on her face because the next thing she knew, Penelope was bearing down on her and pulling her into a tight embrace. With her head buried in her sister's shoulder all Charissa could hear were the gentle words, "I love you. Thank you for protecting my children."

She couldn't stop the flood of tears that came then, flooding her eyes and soaking into Penelope's sweater.

*   *   *

Discussing what to do with Timothy's body was hard. He deserved a good funeral. A final resting place and the dignity that came with it. But with their home surrounded by infected their options were limited in the extreme. They couldn't even get rid of the bodies they didn't want, much less provide for Timothy a fraction of what he deserved.

In the end they settled on moving him into the childrens room, at least there they wouldn't need to sleep beside him and he wouldn't be lumped in with the bodies of his killers. They moved the body of his killer and the first man Charissa had killed into the childrens playroom, it wouldn't be able to function as a good kill point for much longer anyway with how the bodies had been piling up. It was beginning to feel like they had corpses stashed in every room of the house: the play room, kids room, and the basement.

"What are we going to do about our friends?" Penelope asked, looking out at the growing horde. Charissa could see the real concern in her sister's furrowed brow and ached to provide some reasonable solution.

"There are windows on every side of the house on this floor. The best we can do now is use one or two at a time and pick them off in those sections. The kill box is already clogged so that's no help until we can clear it.

Penelope nodded, "That should cut down on their numbers and buy us some time."

Some time for what? Charissa wondered but pushed that thought to the back of her mind. "How are Sophie and Attie doing?"

Penelope sighed and moved away from the window. "Bad. They aren't talking about it, and honestly I don't know if I should make them talk about it. I'm just not equipped for this. Everything else was bad enough but this..." She covered her eyes with her right hand and swallowed before continuing, "as long as we were all together it was okay. Not good, it definitely affected their socialization and growth, but okay. But this? I have no idea if we can recover from this, or if we even should."

"It's a lot." Charissa added.

"Yeah." They sat in silence for a minute just listening to the moans of the dead.

"This wasn't supposed to happen," Penelope whispered, her emotions thickening her voice. "They weren't supposed to deal with stuff like this. And we were both supposed to be there with them." She dropped her head into her hands and her shoulders began to shake.

"Hey, hey, hey," Charissa swooped forward and pulled her older sister into a hug. "You're not alone. I'm here. They'll be okay. They'll be okay." She rubbed circles on Penelope's back and murmured assurances to her despite their possible inaccuracy. Hadn't the past months proven that the future was uncontrollable and unknowable?

Penelope cried herself out in a matter of minutes, pulling back to leave a large damp spot on Charissa's shoulder. "Thanks. We should make food and check on the kids. They've been alone too long." She stood up and set to work. Charissa could see what her sister was doing but also felt inadequate to the task of propping up her sister's mental health while her own was on such a shaky foundation. She looked out the window and recalled her earlier thought patterns.

"I'll make food, you check on the kids." She called out while turning and following her sister.

5

In the moments before minds died the virus plundered. Math, science, music, history; these concepts melded with the experience and instinct of the runners, flyers, and diggers. They enriched the world and brought flashes from the before. Through these it began to piece together its past. Moments in the time before filled in by the ideas and memories of things that hadn't been It but now were.

*   *   *

Dr. Scordato was completely useless. Treegar acknowledged to herself that that wasn't entirely fair. The swelling of his knee had gone down and his foot was looking much better, but experience and the way he winced whenever motion required him to bend his knee or put pressure on the sole of his foot, told Treegar that they would be making absolutely no progress that day.

"Give me your boot." She demanded of him the moment he had finished his breakfast rations.

He turned blurry, sleep filled eyes toward her, "Huh?"

"Give me your boot." She repeated.

"What?"

Perhaps he was still waking up despite having been moving about for the past twenty minutes but he seemed particularly dense today. "Your boot, give it to me."

"Oh, um, okay?" Jason turned back to the tent, returning a

moment later with his boot dangling from his fingertips. The mud and gunk from the previous day's trek had partially dried overnight but still maintained a slimy quality.

Treegar accepted the item, grateful to have her gloves to protect her from whatever clung to the boot. She then turned from Jason and moved to the bank of drawers on the right side of the room. Earlier that morning, while she stood watch and enjoyed the increasing light of dawn, she had opened and assessed the contents of each drawer. Most of them contained a variety of paint and painting equipment, or at least equipment that Treegar assumed was for painting. But one of the drawers contained a selection of glues and tapes. From wood glue to superglue and several that came in two parts and cemented on contact.

She took out the super glue and one of the more full contact cements as well as a roll of duct tape. Then setting them aside, Treegar took the boot to the deep paint splattered sink in the corner of the studio and set to work. She tested the taps first, the hot water tap doing nothing but making an unhealthy sucking noise but once she shut that off and tried the cold water it came out clear. She rinsed the worst of the gunk off, watching as it turned the bottom of the large plastic basin a rich brown, and then dried the boot with a paper towel both inside and out.

With the area as clean and dry as she could make it, Treegar returned where she had left the glue and tape. The cleaning had not revealed some massive hole which she could simply plug up and move on, so Treegar was forced to smooth the sticky super glue over every conceivable place for a leak.

While she worked she listened to her companions plan their next moves.

"We need to find a computer. I'll email Agatha's daughters and let them know we are close. I'm sure they will want to meet with us."

"That sounds like a plan but we don't really know where we are, so are we close? We should prioritize finding out where we are before we get their hopes up." Dr. Nagi countered.

"There is probably a main house not too far from here. We might have seen it last night had it not been so dark when we arrived. I'm sure there will be either a laptop or computer there or at least a way to find out where exactly we are." Garner supplied.

Dr. Scordato's voice was bright in reply, "Then let's go look for it!"

Treegar cut in at that point, having filled every crack on the outside of his boot and set it down to dry. "And what are you going to wear during that journey?"

"Oh, right..." He muttered looking over at her and then down at his exposed foot.

"Garner and I will look for the house. The two of you should remain here and protect our gear." With that decision made she walked toward the entrance and began dismantling her improvised door stops. The knots she'd made took the longest, as her gloves did not allow for the fine motor work that the task required. Finally she pulled out her little knife and put it to good use.

"You know, you might want to leave a little more room for discussion. We aren't a military outfit right now." Garner said softly from behind her.

Treegar grunted but kept her focus on the task at hand. They could talk more freely away from the doctors. Some things had been brewing in the back of her mind for some time and, in light of what just happened to them a day ago, it might just be the right time for her to discuss them with Garner.

She opened the door and welcomed the rush of fresh cold air. Whoever had owned this place had only used a simple latch on the outside to secure the door, clearly break ins weren't a major issue in this area. The rain had washed away much of the snow and brought with it warmer temperatures. There was a temperature gauge on the wall just outside of the building reading a balmy 2 degrees above freezing. Treegar raised an eyebrow at that and considered just what month they were actually in now; it had been so long since she had kept track of that sort of thing. It seemed that at least for now, in this place the grip of winter was loosening. Whether that was a good thing or not she didn't know.

Garner followed her out of the building and joined her in surveying the landscape. The sky continued to weep but now the drops came in a steady steam, pounding away at the remaining drifts of snow. Their path from the previous night was visible as the most clearly washed out portions of the landscape, meandering and inefficient in the extreme.

"Probably shouldn't push into the dark like that again." He commented.

"Yeah." Treegar turned from their trail and took in the rest of their surroundings. There were small groups of trees and the tops of fence posts off to her left while the right seemed to slope away into the distance, whatever might lay in that direction completely obscured by the gray sheets of rain after a dozen feet or so.

She began walking around the building, following the path from the previous night. They rounded the back of the building when a simple two storey farm house came into view. A stone path led from the studio to a set of stairs and a deck. By silent agreement both soldiers began to trudge their way through the snow and mud toward the stairs.

"What's the plan after this?" Treegar broke through their silence, finally addressing the topic which had been plaguing her.

"After?" Garner asked, clearly uncertain as to the parameters of her question.

"After this mission, after we deliver the doctor to his destination. What comes next?"

Garner coughed lightly, as though covering up some other reaction to her clarification. "Well, I'm not sure. I guess we can either stick to the doctors, try to contact the military for further orders, or strike out on our own."

Treegar absorbed those options as they approached the bottom of the stairs. The wood creaked under their boots but most of the snow had already melted and the non-slip material covering the stairs did an excellent job at keeping their feet exactly where they planted them.

"What's your preference?" She kept her voice low and avoided looking into his face by actively peering into the dark interior of the house's windows. The growing morning light served to deepen the shadows inside the building. She crept closer, Garner maintaining position close behind her but never impeding her movements.

"While I enjoy the thought of striking out on our own, we made a commitment to the Canadian Armed Forces and I'd like to at least attempt to report in. It might be good to let the higher ups know what Ward did. They probably won't be able to do anything right now but I want there to be some record of his actions. It wasn't right and he shouldn't get away from it." There was an unexpected level of anger in Garner's voice which almost made Treegar turn from her survey of the house's interior in shock.

She took a calming breath and reached out to test the door, it was unsurprisingly locked.

Despite the naive trust displayed at the studio, it made perfect sense that the door would be locked. She considered breaking one of the large windows that looked out onto the deck but decided to table that idea until she had checked for a spare key. She lifted the welcome mat, nothing. She moved the now dead potted plants and still, nothing. Finally she felt along the top of the door frame, bingo. A tarnished golden key dropped to the deck boards and bounced. The most negative part of her brain imagined it slipping between the boards and getting lost in whatever exists underneath the deck. Thankfully that did not happen. The key bounced twice and landed a few feet away gleaming in the morning light.

Treegar scooped it up and wiggled it into the lock. It stuck and she had to jiggle it firmly before it began to turn, the bolt sliding open with a click. The door swung inward, admitting a band of light into the house that seemed to deepen the shadows. The air was stale and stank of rot. The hair on the back of Treegar's neck stood on end and her instincts screamed that the house held infected.

"Something died here." She said simply, burying her anxiety and taking her first tentative step inside. She took small, careful steps, easing her boots down to limit their sound. Garner moved in behind her, sweeping his gaze over the opposite side of the room but keeping his back close to her own. It was an open sitting room with a small round table, a pair of chairs, and several lamps. The walls were covered in unframed canvases painted in the same style as what Treegar had seen in the studio.

They made their way deeper into the house, stepping out of the spilled light from the door but moving slowly enough that their eyes had plenty of time to adjust to the lower light. The sitting room transitioned into a kitchen with a partial wall and signs of where a set of double doors had once been and had since been removed.

The kitchen had an island in the center, covered in the long forgotten remains of someone's food preparations. Mold now grew in puddles over a cutting board, bowl, and pot with a few scattered droplets of growth around them. Treegar wrinkled her nose but knew that the scent of rot from those particular things would have long since dissipated and that something much larger was the real source of the stench.

Garner followed her lead through the kitchen and into a secondary sitting room, this one dominated by a large flat screen television and a floral print couch. Treegar kept her eyes moving, looking for any sign of an infected, large or small. The longer it took to find what she knew had to be there, the more her stomach knotted up and her senses prickled.

As they rounded the couch, Treegar caught sight of it, not an infected but the purpose of their mission: a laptop. She paused and gestured to it.

Garner nodded and swept down to pick it up as well trace its power cord to where it was plugged into an extension cord. He unplugged it and looped the cord so he could carry it with his free hand. With that task accomplished Treegar released a soft sigh of relief, they might get out of here without a fight.

They retraced their steps, making their way back to the kitchen. They took the shortest route around the island and toward the sitting room. Treegar felt her stomach drop as the floorboards creaked under her weight. She paused, knowing before it even reached her ears what was coming. Still, the replying moan caught her by surprise at how near it was.

Her heart rate picked up and she braced herself for a fight. She ushered Garner past her, toward the door and turned to the source of the moan. There was a door on the other side of the kitchen, beside the stove. It shuddered and shifted, opening inch by inch. Treegar stepped around the island to get a better look. On the floor, wedging the door open was a rotting human arm.

The white of the bone poked out of gangrenous flesh with

yellow and brown bits her mind refused to identify. The fingers skittered and scrapped against the floorboards, dragging the rest behind it and closer to the two soldiers. Despite all she had seen, Treegar felt her stomach roll.

"Let's go." Garner called out. His voice sent the infected arm into a frenzy as it forced more of itself out the door.

Treegar tore her gaze away from the arm and dashed out the door to him. Her skin crawled and the fresh outside air did little to drive away the smell from inside her visor.

6

New populations brought with them new thoughts, memories, and knowledge. They had thought themselves safe from the virus, they were wrong. It knew their fear, understood it in a way that even those who had felt it couldn't,

*   *   *

Jason rubbed his foot anxiously, grateful that he could bend his knee and that his foot no longer retained the dull aching that had interrupted his sleep last night. It was now a normal color and temperature and the swelling in his knee had gone down till it was almost the same size as his other one. Walking was still tender and neither part of his leg wanted to accept his weight but Jason felt an itch to continue moving. Maybe it was the rain but he felt like they were finally approaching their destination.

The past months had been filled with abject failure on his part and he was desperate to finally succeed at something, even if it was just granting his friend this one small request. Jason slowly lowered his foot back down and picked up his still damp and smelly sock. He needed to find a way to dry it out before they set out or his foot would be back where it was last night. Maybe they could find a pharmacy and get more socks? Or a foot fungus cream? There had to be more of them as they came closer to civilization.

They had taken down the tent and repacked all the gear and now waited for the soldiers to return with nothing more to do except watch and wait.

"They're on their way back." Jaspreet called out from where

she had been watching the house through one of the studio windows.

Jason hobbled over to her, trying to keep his limp to a minimum. "Did they find anything?" The question became redundant the moment he could see for himself. Garner strode confidently down the slight hill with an older laptop and a coiled up cable clutched to his chest and protected from the rain. "Yahtzee." Jason fist pumped the air, uncool though he knew that action to be.

"This could be it." Jaspreet turned to him with a small smile.

"Or at least the beginning of it," Jason rejoined with a smile of his own. It was too early to really celebrate, heaven knew he'd learned the folly of premature celebration. Having a way to communicate not only with Penelope and Charissa but with the wider world would mean everything. It meant that he could find out how the international efforts to find a cure were coming along. It would literally put him back on the map, not only scientifically, but in the practical sense of knowing where they were and how much further they needed to travel.

They waited until the soldiers rounded the studio and then hastily unblocked the door and opened it for their companions.

"That was reckless." Garner scolded them.

"We could see it was you." Jaspreet countered cheekily.

He snorted, "and if we had been infected?"

"Pfft." She scoffed, "infected don't carry laptops like that."

Garner laughed at this logic and rejoined, "and how do they carry laptops, doctor?"

Jason shook his head at their exchange and quietly relieved Garner of the aforementioned laptop. He moved off to the corner while Jaspreet began a silly impression of a classic zombie-like creature carrying a laptop and moaning words like "eeeeemaaaailll" and ssssssynnnnerrrgyyy". Jason chuckled at their antics and said a small prayer of thanks that they felt safe enough for such levity.

He sat on one of the cupboards and opened the laptop and turned it on. The screen lit up and stayed exactly the same for so long that Jason began to wonder if the thing actually worked. Finally the screen changed marking a precedent which ran true for the entire start up, with each stage taking infinitely longer than he had patience for.

When the computer finally settled into the login page his heart sank. Right, passwords, that was a normal thing and something he should have expected but also had no skills to get around. Hesitantly he used the touchpad to click on the user name, 'Maggie'.

The expected password line did not appear and the computer just resumed its lengthy start up process. Apparently 'Maggie' hadn't bothered with a password and Jason could not thank her enough for it. The background was of a beautiful sunset with an island silhouetted in the foreground and surrounding ocean a gorgeous cerulean. The icons popped slowly into place in neat columns on the left side of the screen.

It automatically connected to the internet and Jason couldn't believe their luck. Was this the universe balancing for their bad luck of getting captured the other day or would a higher price be demanded in the future? He shook off that sense of foreboding and sent a silent prayer of thanks for their current good fortune.

The internet browser took just as long to load as the startup had and Jason wondered if that was due to poor computer maintenance, age, or the result of being left to sit for the past several months.

While he waited, Jaspreet and Garner continued to rib

each other in more and more ridiculous ways. Treegar was characteristically stoic and silent, which Jaosn considered simply inhuman considering the antics of their companions. She caught him watching and strode over to where he was sitting.

"How's it coming along?" The question felt more like a demand. Like she was questioning what was taking him so long and Jason bristled at the implication that he was being slow deliberately. Didn't she know that he was just as eager as her to get moving?

"This thing's a piece of junk," he explained, "took until just now to boot up and open a web browser." He waited for some condescending or skeptical retort but what he got instead was:

"Understood. I'd like us to remain here tonight. Your leg needs rest and there is no sense in setting out until we have a firm understanding of where we are and where we are heading."

Jason balked at the idea, "stay? My leg is fine." He knew that to be untrue but couldn't stand the thought that his injuries were the reason for delaying their journey.

"It is not. Your ligaments will take weeks to fully recover, if they ever do."

"Weeks!" He gasped.

"We will not wait here that long. We need only wait for the information we seek. I assume that the laptop does not have cellular data capabilities. Leaving before we receive a response would be counterproductive and might cause Mrs. Abernathy's children undue worry."

Jason pursed his lips and conceded that point. "You are correct. I had not thought that far ahead. It would be wise to give them a chance to respond before leaving." In his annoyance he fell into a more formal cadence of speaking, leaning into the formality and politeness to avoid snapping at the woman. It was incredible how she could completely crush his jovial mood.

She gave him a sharp nod, pivoted on her heel and walked away toward the back of the studio. With the tent down the space looked far too large for just one artist, the lone easle seeming to draw the soldiers attention.

Jason tore his eyes from her retreating back and refocused on reaching his email. Their conversation had allowed time for the browser to fully load and it sat patiently for his direction. Navigating between websites took longer than he would have liked but it was a matter of seconds rather than minutes now. Reaching his email brought with it both a sense of relief and one of anticipation. Despite the dozens of unopened emails he immediately clicked the 'compose' button and began writing to Agatha's daughters.

Penelope and Charissa,

I regret to inform you of your mother's passing.

Jason cursed and tried to think of some other way to start this email but none came. That was the crux of the situation, the most important and devastating information he needed to deliver. He drew in a shuddering breath and plowed on.

I wish that I could have informed you sooner but events transpired which prevented communication. You may be comforted to know that she passed in her sleep, in relative comfort. She was a pleasure to know and I regret...

He paused and back tracked, the girls didn't need to hear his litany of regrets, not even when it came to their mother.

She was a pleasure to know and all who knew her were grateful that they did.

Prior to her passing she requested that her rings be returned to the two of you. This is my secondary purpose in reaching out to you at this time. I have your mothers rings in my possession and wish to pass them along to you. For this purpose, I and three of my colleagues have traveled south.

Agatha told me roughly where I could find you, however a more accurate address or appropriate meeting place would be necessary if I am to fulfill this task. If you would reply with one of these, I would be most grateful.

I am so sorry for your loss and hope to hear back from you soon.

Dr. Jason Scordato

He clicked send and sat back. That was one of the most difficult emails he had ever written and he felt like an absolute prat for relying on so much formal language but after shifting into it during his exchange with Treegar, he had been unable to break out of it for the email. But it was sent and that was all there was. Now they just had to wait, and as Treegar said, heal.

7

It glutted itself on new minds, driving the fresh bodies in a fervor, understanding their fragility as it couldn't have had when it was still young. It had learned the consequences of time and knew the only escape lay in growth.

*   *   *

The second day after Timothy's death was both harder and easier. Easier in that they hadn't slept in a room with his corpse and thus were all better rested. Harder in that emotions which had been numbed with exhaustion now found strength in rest.

Infected still pounded on the house, the collective noise drawing more to the horde. Each wall had at least a dozen infected and rotting bodies slamming into it in a mindless attempt to reach the few living inside. Dozens of human bodies.

Charissa wondered when that had changed, when had the infected stopped being mainly rats, cats, and dogs who would scratch and chew at their siding? When had they become almost solely humans? Were there even any uninfected animals left?

The human infected clawed ineffectually at the siding and used their bodies as battering rams. The acid exuding from their skid probably did more damage than their pounding and even then it only affected the few areas unprotected by vinyl siding. She was grateful that she and Timothy had covered all the windows and doors with stolen siding.

Reaching the infected from the second floor windows came in various levels of difficulty. None were as easy as the front room but it wasn't difficult to lure infected around the house to the windows which allowed for better accessibility. One look at her or Penelope and the whole horde would converge on their location. Shambling, stumbling, and surging until they were crawling over each other to reach them.

The children were unfortunately left in the bedroom, with the television serving as babysitter. Neither Charissa or Penelope felt good about that decision but with the constant threat that the infected posed, It wasn't practical for one of them to step away and sit with them for the whole day. They took breaks, switching out every hour or two to use the bathroom, eat something, and check on Sophia and Atticus, but for that day that was the best they could manage.

As the day became too dark to see, she and Penelope closed the windows and pulled back to the main bedroom. Sophia and Atticus were absorbed in a brightly colored cartoon but flinched when the door opened. Charissa's heart ached as they clung to each other for the brief moment before they recognized that it was her and their mother entering the room. The moment only emphasized how truly not okay they both were.

She slipped back out of the room and went to the kitchen for some food. The cupboards were half bare but several cans of ready to eat pork and beans seemed like the best of the bad options. She briefly thought about cooking a real meal, turning on the oven and baking a casserole or a whole chicken. Something fragrant and extravagant. It wasn't like they were hiding any longer. The horde at their doors was a clear declaration that there were people here, but the horde also served as temporary protection from any further raiders.

But her arms were sore and tired and she would rather shower and sleep than spend at least half an hour in the semi darkness cooking. Maybe she'd do that tomorrow.

The cans of beans were welcomed back in the bedroom and

space was made for her under the blankets. Cans were shared and the four watched the kids cartoon. Charissa let herself relax into their tiny oasis, ignoring the looming shadow of the grief and trauma that kept the kids from laughing.

Sophia snuggled into her side and Charissa wrapped an arm around her niece. The cartoon was one she wasn't familiar with, the kids having completely blown through anything she knew in the past months and returned to some of their newer favorites for what to them was nostalgic comfort. She picked up her phone from the side table and unlocked it, pausing for a moment before opening her mailbox and taking a look at the 38 unopened emails it claimed to hold.

Above the scads of automatic emails and general junk was one from Jason Scordato. Charissa remembered that that was the same man who claimed to be her mothers doctor and a deep sense of apprehension settled into her gut.

She let her hand drop to her lap and stared at the cartoon. It took her till the end of the episode before she convinced herself to actually open the email. Mom's last email had sounded an awful lot like goodbye and within the first line of Dr. Scordato's Charissa knew that her gut feeling had been right.

Mom was gone.

She didn't cry. There had been enough tears in the past few days and this news, while it ached, was neither unexpected nor shocking. Somehow, it was a relief to know that mom wasn't suffering anymore. She knew how much pain she'd been in before she left and that pain had been managed by drugs, what must it have been like once those drugs ran out? It was better that Mom didn't feel like that anymore.

She slid down and snuggled into Sophia, pulling her little body closer to her side and steeled herself for the rest of the email. When she was ready she turned away from the others and reopened her phone reading over the remaining paragraphs.

Her rings? This man had traveled, what even was the distance between his mysterious facility and here? Whatever, he had traveled who knew how far to deliver Mom's rings to her and Penelope. During the apocalypse. He was insane.

Charissa let out a huff and then a chuckle and finally a nearly silent belly laugh that turned into full body sobbing. She completely lost control of her emotions and could feel Sophia reaching her short arms around her and Penelope stroking the uncovered parts of her back. She felt like she was losing her mind. Mom was gone. Timothy was gone. The world had ended. And this crazy man had traveled hundreds of kilometers like it was no big deal. And now he wanted to meet but didn't know where to actually go! It was ridiculous, who would do that?

Out of breath and warmed by the exertion of laughing, Charissa reopened her phone, pushed herself to sit up and passed her phone to Penelope. Penelope accepted the phone and looked down at it with a concerned furrow to her brow.

Sophia and Atticus looked between their mother and their aunt while Penelope scrolled through and read the doctors email. "Oh," she sighed before handing the phone back, "We should discuss that later." Then she turned back to the show and pretended like what had happened wasn't that big of a deal.

*　　*　　*

"So, what do you think?" Penelope opened the discussion. They were standing side by side just about to start picking off infected for the day and it took Charissa a moment to figure out what Penelope meant.

"About the doctor? I honestly don't know. I want moms rings, but are they really worth the risk? He's obviously insane just for doing this, so how can we really trust him? I just don't know."

"Mmm…" Penelope hummed and then took a moment to slam her spear into the head of an infected. She wrenched it free and sighed.

"I think it would be a mistake to distrust him based on the actions of other people. Mom trusted him. At least I believe she did by her last email. He claims that she entrusted him with this task and while I have no idea how he managed to get here, the fact that he has followed through on that trust shows that he is worthy of it. Besides, we are vulnerable. What happened just proves that we need more numbers, people we trust who will protect us and the kids."

Charissa neutralized an infected while she pondered her sister's words, "So, you want to tell him where we are? Invite him and his group in?"

Penelope shrugged, "maybe. But we shouldn't make snap decisions. Think on it and we can email him tonight. If he's come as far as he says, he can wait a day for our answer."

8

In blood and brains the virus surged forth, spreading through both heat and cold. It encompassed. With each new life gained it both expanded and contracted. It felt something imminent. Something spoke to it of change. It shaped the world but that sense of foreboding drove it further. It could sense the vibrancy of youth fading and something known and unknown looming on its horizon.

*   *   *

Dr. Scordato obsessively refreshed his inbox for what had to be the fiftieth time in the past hour. Treegar turned away from him and took one more leisurely lap around the studio. The space was well lit despite the sunlight being heavily diluted through layers of clouds and constant rain. The drops created a relaxing patter on the roof and she could feel that sound working to ease the tension inside her.

She huffed a little at herself, it had been a long time since she had felt any kind of safety and yet, in this mostly glass building, with a confirmed infected little more than a stone's throw away, the simple sound of rain on a roof was tricking her mind into feeling safe. It was ridiculous, but she was okay with it.

What she wasn't okay with were the results of her conversation with Garner. The loyal part of her knew that checking in was the right thing to do. They had sworn oaths, signed contracts, and hadn't yet finished serving their time. But returning to the military structure meant a number of things that made her uneasy. There would be psychological evaluations; which she doubted she would pass. There would be medical check ups; and after the one performed by Dr. Rudolph, she didn't know if she could undergo one of those again. Worst of all, they would definitely separate her from Garner.

That more than anything informed her unilateral command that they remain here until Mrs. Abernathy's daughters replied. The reasons she had given the doctor were no less valid for this separate selfish one.

This line of thinking was bringing the tension back and she didn't want that. She pushed the thoughts away and focused on the soft patter of rain. The gentle music as it impacted the roof, countered by the heavy drips from the eaves and the resultant splashes in the puddles. All of it combined into a white noise which set her mind, if not her heart, at ease.

"So, I hear we're staying?"

Treegar startled a little and then relaxed again when her mind caught up with her reflexes. "It is our most reasonable choice. It would be counterproductive to leave before we have a better understanding of our course."

Vincent nodded, missing the lies behind her logic, his eyes crinkling with a repressed smile. "That's very reasonable. And my earlier comment about discussing these kinds of things?" That last part was layered with both humor and censure sending heat to stain her cheeks.

She turned to face the nearest window and trusted that the angle and her visor would hide her emotions. "You are correct. Though my logic is sound, I should have considered the input of the group. Would you have us do something different?"

Now Vincent laughed, "Wow, what a spot on Vulcan impression. Spock would be impressed."

Madison tilted her head in confusion, that was a Star Trek thing, right? "I'm not sure I understand."

He waved his hand at her, dismissing the question, "It doesn't matter. No, I wouldn't have us do anything different. We absolutely should stay here until we know where we are heading next. Besides, we've been going straight for…" He pauses and counts off fingers before dropping his hands and continuing, "I honestly have no idea, but a day or two of rest will do us good. Particularly the doctor, I hate to think how the old guy's leg is going to heal once we are walking again."

Treegar nodded, but remained silent.

"But that's not the point. The point is," he paused to draw in a long breath, "you and I aren't the leaders here. We aren't captains who just issue orders and expect everyone to obey. The doctors aren't our subordinates and we can't treat them as such. They have really improved since we've been out here and they have education and skills that neither of us have. You have to treat them as equals and ask for their input. You have no idea what they might add to the discussion."

He made good points, but it was so much simpler to just tell them what to do. And with how scared they were of her, they never argued. Discussion would just take longer and break down that barrier of fear. She felt like she needed that barrier, though she couldn't quite name why.

"That takes so much longer. " She whined and then realized what she had done and snapped her mouth shut to prevent any other such juvenile and petulant outbursts.

Garner laughed and moved closer to her, until the edge of his protective jacket was pressing into her own, "You might not like it, but it could be useful. Besides, wouldn't it be better if we could act as a real team?"

She pressed her lips together and tried to allow his proximity to distract her. They were already a real team, at least she and Garner were. The scientists were more like cargo.

"Come on, at least think about it. I'm going to take this opportunity to clean up a little. Do you mind watching my six while I make use of our luxurious bathing facilities?" It took her a moment to comprehend that he meant the sink in the back of the room and then it hit her that he would be washing in ice cold water.

She chuckled, certain that his little clean up would be very refreshing. "Sure, let's go."

*   *   *

Jaspreet was worried. Not about their current situation, though that certainly warranted some worry, but about what came next. She had always been a planner, that was what got her through school and the infancy of her career. That impulse had been stymied in the past few months with the world falling apart and her future looking both very short and very uncomfortable. But she was nearly within throwing distance of home and somehow that made her more rather than less anxious.

According to google maps, which hopefully remained fairly accurate, they were just south of a town called Lytton. All things considered "Salvation" was probably what was left of that community. But that brought them a few days, maybe a week, from Agatha's daughters and the completion of this particular mission. What came after that was the true source of her worries.

She looked around at her companions, laughing at a shirtless Garner as he flinched and hissed from the cold water. She hadn't seen so much skin in ages and it made her rather prudishly uncomfortable. Treegar seemed to have no trouble averting her gaze from her partner, though Jaspreet knew there were more than platonic feelings between them. On Garner's side this had manifested in a certain softness toward the other soldier, not a softness that assumes Treegar required protection but more one which meant that Garner felt protected by Treegar. For Treegar's part it was more obvious, of their group the only one she seemed comfortable with was Garner. Jaspreet stood watch many nights bearing witness to the ease with which the soldiers slept in one another's arms.

Jason was being an idiot, again. Sometimes she wondered if the man was forty-five or fourteen. She honestly didn't know if he was forty-five though she doubted he was younger. Regardless of his chronological age, he was sulking and obsessing with all the hormonal vigor of a pubescent. It was the joy of Jaspreets life that she had never been saddled with one of her own. Hundreds of people had warned her that she would regret that but looking at the man-baby mumbling to himself and fiddling with the laptop made her wonder at those peoples' sanity. At least this child wasn't her responsibility.

That thought brought her back around to her worry. What should she do after they complete Jason's mission?

Home was Victoria, Vancouver Island. But after so long away, with all that had happened, was it worth it to traverse the strait? She had no idea if that was even possible for her. She hadn't been in a boat smaller than a ferry in years and not on one in the ocean for many years before that. Jaspreet had the distinct memory of seasickness and had to stop thinking about it before her memory affected her well being.

They had been relying so much on Garner and Treegar the past weeks that the thought of setting out on her own seemed like suicide. She resolved then to try and do more, learn more, and be less of a burden during the next few days. Anything to better prepare her for whatever was coming next.

9

There was a moment, a single second of pure existential terror, which sent the virus scrambling back in a million places all at once. In the wake the virus searched for the source of the fear and found something that troubled it more than anything. It found nothing. No memory, no inciting incident, no fire, no death, simply nothing.

* * *

Jason spent a fitful night listening to his companions breathe. He drifted in his mind for a while, wondering about the natural selection qualities of sleep noises. How many people had been given a premature death due to their snoring keeping their companions awake? The thought swirled around in his mind until the pale light of dawn lit the inside of his eyelids.

What followed was another day of waiting. After all, as he was reminded, there was no point in leaving till they had received an answer. While he waited, he used the supremely slow laptop to check in on scientific forums and see where the research community was currently.

While many interesting theories were thrown about, Jason had expected to feel more lost in the discourse. He had been separated from it for some weeks now with spotty participation prior to that due to his own research and attempts to fulfill as many testing requests as Jaspreet and his teams could manage. Unfortunately, the community seemed to have entered a loop with very little actual progress being made.

Some researchers had shared about their success in accessing, on a limited scale, something they referred to as an on/off switch in Xeno-1. Unfortunately, they weren't willing to share their methods yet as they were preparing a paper to publish on it. A paper. Jason had to shake his head, no matter what the emergency, academia would have its way.

Another group insisted that Xeno-1 had a language and could be communicated with. They used nearly anecdotal evidence indicating a hive mind and more evidentiary collections of the tonation of individual moans as reference for their research positing that sufficient moans were recorded and then given context a database of translation might be assembled. They even theorized that it might actually require looking at the layering of several creatures moaning to determine linguistic meaning. All that being said, it was an interesting theory but Jason had heard enough infected moans to doubt the veracity of these ideas.

Most unfortunately, it seemed that no progress had been made in the effort to find a cure. He scrolled back through the discussions and found that such efforts had been thoroughly derailed by the sudden vocalization of the infected. The unexplained shift from silent killing machines to moaning monsters had sent researchers veering off track into a million rabbit holes to determine the cause.

Once he knew this, Jason set about writing a brief but detailed account of his and Dr. Nagi's experience with the lattice structure and how breaking it might be the catalyst for the change. He sincerely hoped that holding that particular answer would encourage his better situated colleagues to resume their research into a cure.

He then navigated to the news and spent a short time reading out bits of global news. There was almost nothing coming out of Canada or America, both countries being bogged down in the fight against the infected with no official journalism on anything else. South America was being overrun as well and there were reports of Japan and China shutting down due to their own infected populations. Both countries were keeping their numbers and details underwraps but Jason saw several news outlets catastrophizing their severity.

Most distressing were reports of North Korea getting their hands on Xeno-1 and deploying it in some sort of viral gun to expand their borders. They had attacked South Korea with it but the situation rapidly got out of hand because now both countries were on full quarantine lockdown.

The tide of infection seemed relentless in sweeping around the globe. So far Europe, Africa, and Australasia were mostly safe but the progress of Xeno-1 made the eventual infection of those areas seem inevitable.

At that point he navigated away from the news, too overwhelmed to process it all. Everything was bad. When he'd been doing research there had been a sense that he was participating in the solution, small though his contribution seemed and frustrating as that might have been. When they'd been traveling he'd been too tired and grief stricken to think beyond the next step. Taking this moment to rest merely allowed the rest of the world to rush in and leave him utterly helpless and useless. All of his efforts hadn't amounted to a single thing in the grand scheme of this emergency. Jaspreet had contributed more and she worked with stars and rocks. He was the virologist, what use had he been?

He clicked back to the tab for his inbox and refreshed the page. Nothing.

He closed the laptop and began to pace the room, his recovering and stiff legs protesting each and every step. Jaspreet was taking a nap in the tent while both Garner and Treegar were sitting and staring out the studio windows. They each turned and gave him partial attention as his movements brought him near but neither engaged him in conversation.

Why weren't the sisters responding? Were they dead? Was this whole thing pointless? What would he do if they were? What happened then?

The pacing expended some of his nervous energy but also created something of a feedback loop in his thoughts. His pace grew faster and faster until he was nearly jogging around the tent, arms swinging wildly with manic energy.

"You okay there, bud?" Garner broke through the silence.

Jason grunted and continued his circling.

Garner turned to Treegar and gave her some kind of look, Jason didn't catch it but also didn't want to know. He knew he looked crazy. Maybe they were contemplating putting him out of his misery. After all, with the sisters not replying their mission was basically already over and while they had agreed to take him this far, they hadn't said anything about what would happen after.

Instead of a swift bullet to his brain, Garner chose to stand and join Jason in his pacing. "This waiting can drive you kinda loopy, right?" The soldier looked over at Jason as though expecting a certain reaction, "Get it? Loopy, cause you're walking in circles." He then sighed, "Look, I get it. But we've got a good place to wait it out. We are even relatively safe. They might not be in a space where they can check their email everyday. Or maybe they checked it and are considering what to do. You can't blame them for wanting to think a minute."

Jason sighed and slowed his pace a little. Garner adjusted his steps to match after only a second placing the soldier slightly ahead of Jason for several paces. "I know, it's just..." he took a deep breath, "I'm not sure they'll ever reply. What if they're dead? What if this whole thing has been a colossal waste of your time?" He stopped and turned to the window. His leg aches just above the knee so he shifts his weight off that leg and onto the other. The rain ran in little streams down the glass, clustering into drops before submitting to gravity and sliding down.

"Then we find a good place and hunker down. Maybe contact the military and see if we can check back in. We're all here because of them, they might be doing something to control all of this. Just because we were stuck while up north doesn't mean it's the same down here. And if it is and we are on our own, what does that change? Nothing." Garner touched Jason's arm, the large glove applying a comforting pressure through all of the layers. "If they are gone, then they are already with Agatha. She wouldn't hold that against you. We made the best time we could to get down here. If something happened in the meantime then that is out of our hands. We can only do what we can do." With that comforting fatalism, he began to turn away. "How about I open up a can and we all eat something?"

Jason huffed a laugh, "Sure, sounds good." Garner had a way of siphoning off all the anxiety Jason created and making it seem either reasonable or unnecessary. The man was truly something.

*   *   *

There was no response by the time it became too dark to safely keep the brightly lit computer screen on. With more than a little regret and impatience Jason closed the laptop and went to bed.

The morning broke with rays of light piercing the still glistening windows and refracting throughout the studio. It made the walls of the tent glow. Jason cracked his eyes open and for a brief moment, while his mind was still waking up, felt peace. He lingered in that feeling, absorbing the glowing light of the tent walls through his visor and drifted on just the edge of consciousness.

The rustling of the morning watch and soft conversation slowly drew him out of that peaceful moment.

"Shouldn't be more than four or five days." Came Jaspreets voice, gently tinged with what sounded like hope.

"I'd count on six, though I am glad we shouldn't need a boat or anything. That would be tricky to find." That voice was deeper, probably belonging to Garner.

Jason tried to determine context from just those two comments but his sleep muddled mind was having trouble making connections.

"At least the weather has cleared."

"Just look at that sunrise!"

"I'm glad they are willing to meet. I don't know what Jason would do if..."

"I was worried about that too."

Treegar let out a soft snort and rolled over in her sleep. Jason blinked rapidly and shook his head a little to speed up his sluggish neurons. What had he heard? A trip of four to six days. They were willing to meet.

He sat straight up and then had to sink back down as his brain fuzzed and his vision blurred. The sisters had replied. They were willing to meet. They will be there in less than a week!

Jason smiled and then let out a soft silent chuckle. After a moment of silent celebration, he made gentler moves toward disengaging himself from his blanket and exiting the tent.

10

The mysteries and worries had begun to multiply, fear and memories eliciting unwanted reactions beyond the virus' control. It became in that uncertainty more volatile, stretching and seeking, pounding and hunting, throwing itselves after prey as though by growing it could eliminate those feelings and escape what was coming.

*   *   *

Greg ran his hands over his face in a futile attempt at rubbing away the sleepiness that felt like a permanent part of him. All day, everyday, it was report after report, all saying essentially the same thing. Nothing. But he had to read them. That was after all his job. Especially now, when the fate of the country, and probably the world, might reside in one of those emails.

With a sigh he dropped his hands, grabbed his mug of steaming water, they had run through the city's entire store of both coffee and tea so until things settled down enough to reestablish supply chains this was the best he was going to get. If past experience had shown anything, it was that supply chains do not easily shut down and then reopen. Even if they could get a handle on this Virus and reopen things tomorrow, it would be years before he saw another coffee bean.

Still, the hot water was better than nothing. With winter weather affecting public services and the maintenance people unable to safely leave their homes to fix breakdowns, it was a small miracle that Greg's government office had power for lights, his computer and the slowly failing heat. The hot water helping to warm him from the stomach out was much better than slowly losing the feeling in his fingers.

After a few sips he pulled the mug to his chest with his left hand and used his right to click open the next report. It hailed from a private conglomerate research group based in Milan but composed of scientists from across the world.

Results of Trials 367b

Summary: Viral agent can be deactivated through application of near infrared light conducted in laboratory settings.

Greg paused after that stunning first sentence, stunning by research paper standards not regular person standards. It could be turned off, deactivated. They might have some way to shut Xeno-1 down!

He leaned in and began a more enthusiastic reading than he had begun with. By the end of the report he felt both invigorated and a little disappointed. They could turn the virus off, in small amounts, within a confined space, and with fairly specialized technology. It wasn't the cure he had been hoping for, it wasn't even a viable method of combating the spread, but it was something. With enough time and resources maybe it could become a cure.

*　　*　　*

It wasn't even dawn yet but both Penelope and Charissa were awake. They stared at each other over the tops of Atticus and Sophia's heads, raising eyebrows and making faces. The whole thing was reminiscent of their sleepovers as children and gave Charissa a sense of nostalgic security that she knew to be false.

They had replied to Dr. Scordato late last night but the decision to do so had not come easily to either of them. Though they had only discussed it in dribs and drabs throughout the day, Charissa knew they both had serious concerns that they'd needed to wrestle with. For her part, Timothy's final request of her weighed heavily into why they shouldn't reply. How would inviting four strangers to their home factor into protecting Sophia and Atticus? On the one hand, they could be dangerous just as Ryosuke's group had proven to be. On the other, they could be good allies, having a doctor would greatly improve the children's long term chances and clearly the group knew how to survive in the chaos out there, something that they would all eventually need to learn as Charissa did not see a way for the situation to get better in the immediate future.

Deciding to send that email came more down to Penelope's hopes than Charissa's concerns. Penelope didn't want her children to fear strangers. She wanted them to know that just because they didn't know someone yet didn't make that person an enemy. Charissa could understand that desire, the way Atticus and Sophia reacted whenever the door was opened was upsetting enough and how they required hand holding when going to the bathroom was worse.

They had cleaned the door and the floor in the bedroom and hallway today, using every cleaner in the house to try and remove the stains left from the pooled and dried blood. Charissa imagined that if they had acted more immediately the marks would be less permanent, but even with their best efforts dark patches and lines remained where fluids had seeped into and become a part of the boards.

There had been the hope that without those reminders the kids would feel safer moving throughout the house on their own again, in the hours between cleaning and falling asleep that had not proven true but it was too soon to tell if it would help in the long run..

The dim halflight of various plugged in electronic devices gave the sisters strange orange and blue planes to their faces. Something of her thoughts must have shown on her face because Penelope's brow furrowed and she mouthed "are you okay?"

Charissa forced a smile and slightly nodded, mouthing "breakfast" before slipping one leg at a time out from the blankets and letting the rest of her body slide over the edge as well. The room was chilly compared to the cuddly warmth of the bed so she pulled a sweater off the top of a pile of clothes and slipped it over top of the rest of her clothing. The extra insulation it provided was more imagined than actual but it made her feel better regardless.

She made her way out of the bedroom. The infected had spent the night buffeting away at the house and she knew that the interior walls would need to be checked for possible weak points. Before, well not before everything went to crap because it had started well after that but before Timothy died, they had checked the walls just about everyday, patching up the occasional hole and ensuring a certain level of peace of mind. She mentally counted the days and was shocked to realize how little time had passed. She counted again, pausing before the kitchen standing in the center of the stain left by the first person she had killed. Time had become such a whirlpool of grief, duty, and comfort that it had lost previous markers of significance. That day itself seemed to exist in a liminal space outside of her normal concept of time.

She stepped off of the stain and into the kitchen, picking up the can opener from the counter and opening the cupboard to see what was still available up here. There was a can of vegetable soup, the kind with alphabet noodles that she remembered enjoying as a kid. That found its way into her hand and before she knew what she was doing it was half opened. It dropped in two chunks into a microwavable bowl. She gave it a little shake to dislodge the last bits and then set the can aside and put the bowl in the microwave for two minutes. She watched the illuminated window as the bowl rotated and the numbers counted down. At three she lifted her hand to the button for the door and stopped the countdown by opening it.

The contents were steaming and the sides hot so Charissa wrapped her hands in the sleeves of her outermost sweater and pulled it out, setting down on the counter and digging a spoon out of the drawer. She stirred it and took a tentative bite. The center hadn't been warmed but the outer edges had been near boiling so combined they were a comfortable eating temperature, if not as warm as she usually liked the first few bites of soup. But then, she hadn't added any water to the concentrated soup so it had warmed to more of a stew consistency.

She ate half of the bowl before the pit in her stomach claimed to be full and set the bowl back down. Despite having been drawn to the soup by nostalgia, the soup tasted both bland and salty. She walked away from the half eaten bowl, reminding herself to go back for it and possibly offer it to the children, maybe it was better suited to childish palates.

Charissa wasn't worried about the walls and windows on this floor, after the birds had stopped dive bombing them there hadn't been much wear and tear this high up. So, she made her way down the stairs, past the front door. It was still closed though she wanted to fix and reinforce the lock on it so they weren't depending on her improvised wedge under the door knob. It was good planning that made the door harder for the infected to access due to the barriers they'd placed outside to usher them into the kill zone. Without that, the constant pounding would certainly have broken the chair that held the door closed.

She moved past the chair and down the stairs to the basement, flipping on the light to see where she was going. A wave of something hit her; fear, anxiety, and something she had no name for; they stopped her in her tracks, sending her straight down. She dropped on to the step and looked down at the unmoving corpses. Blood had long since pooled and despite the cold was beginning to dry. The bright red of fresh blood had shifted into something darker.

The hairs on her arms stood up and a shudder ripped through her. She pulled in a shallow breath and tried to force control over her body. It didn't work. Her eyes stung and her face grew hot while her body grew cold. She had killed those people. They were dead because of her. Another shudder tore through her and a moment later she was sobbing into her knees.

The rational part of her mind told her that what she had done was necessary, that they had attacked and she had only defended. It didn't make it any easier. She had taken lives and she felt the cost of those actions on her soul.

Slowly the tears stopped on their own, not because the pain was gone but because her eyes had run dry. Sobs pulled from her throat for another minute but they too eventually subsided. Her body finally became too numb to overwhelm her.

Charissa leaned forward and rocked her stiffening body off the stair and down the rest of them. She didn't want to leave the bodies as they were, Sophia and Atticus shouldn't see this and she didn't want to look at them this way again. Hesitantly she reached down and grasped the flung out wrist of the woman at the bottom of the stairs. The skin was cold and the arms stiff. Charissa flinched back and then turned to the side. Everything she had recently eaten came spewing out.

Barely digested chunks of vegetable soup landed with a splat on the ground. The orange broth mixed with yellow stomach acid to create a sickening sunrise on the floor. She pulled back and heaved again and again, her stomach revolting against what she was asking her body to do.

Eventually that too ran its course. She was able to wipe away the corners of her mouth and stand back up. Instead of returning to the task of moving bodies she walked away and found her work gloves. If she was going to force herself to move bodies, at least she didn't have to actually touch them.

The gloves were cold and stiff but quickly softened and warmed with her hands inside them. Wearing them made the act of reaching down and grabbing the corpses arms slightly less revolting. She strained and twitched, bracing her feet against the floor as best she could to gain traction. For a long minute she pulled and pulled, pitting the entirety of her weight against that of the corpse with nothing happening. Slowly, with the sound of something wet and sticky coming unstuck, the body began to shift.

One small step at a time, Charissa slowly moved the woman's body from the bottom of the stairs and slid it deeper into the basement. It wasn't perfect but at least it moved her out of immediate sight. Her body shook with the effort and her many layers felt entirely too warm but at least that one trigger was no longer waiting at the bottom of the stairs.

The remaining bodies were larger and heavier than the first. Charissa shied past Ryosuke's body and went for the other man's. After grunting and straining against his dead weight until she felt like even in the cold she was overheating, she gave up. Both he and Ryosuke would have to wait until she had Penelope there to help her.

She took a deep breath and waited for her heart rate to settle back down. When she was ready she began to walk the inside of the outer walls, looking for signs that the infected were wearing through. While the human's throwing themselves at the walls didn't break through the way the rats and smaller animals had, there were still weak points.

She came across one such weak point in the southernmost corner of the basement. Fluid, she assumed from the piled up infected outside, had worked its way through the layers of siding that she, Penelope, and Timothy had used to cover a hole and was seeping into the basement. She kept well away from the growing puddle and grabbed a jug of bleach off the storage shelves. Dumping it in a ring around the puddle seemed like the best option for that kind of incursion. What she hadn't counted on was the simply terrific combination of smells that would produce. Human decay plus vomit plus bleach equals something eyewatering that made her lungs feel as though the air itself was attacking her.

She gasped and coughed, backing away through the basement and to the stairs as quickly as her legs could carry her. She crawled up the steps on her hands and knees until the overwhelming odor finally began to fade. It still felt like her nose and mouth had been coated by it but her lungs no longer burned.

Feeling somewhere between an idiot and a nincompoop though she couldn't currently put a finger on why, Charissa made her way back up the rest of the stairs and down the hall to the bedroom, hoping that Penelope wouldn't laugh at her grotesque comedy of errors.

11

Most of it focused on growth, surging forward to outrun the fear. But part of it, a piece that could not let go, probed. It poked and prodded at the fear, turning it over and discovering... not the source but another ancient memory, something important, something from before.

*   *   *

Treegar woke up in the middle of a planning meeting. She had taken the middle shift that night and while her sleep had been broken it had at least been dreamless. Her companions all sat about discussing what she assumed would be their next steps while she worked to achieve her normal level of functionality. It wasn't easy but cold water and nibbling a granola bar helped.

While she ate and drank, Garner summarized their decisions, informing her that the sisters had responded and that they could reach them in under a week. Then the discussion turned to supply management which gave Treegar's sluggish mind a chance to process what she had just been told.

They were leaving today, and probably very soon. The knowledge twisted her stomach into knots and almost sent the water and hard lumps of granola up and out. She swallowed the nausea and chased it with another sip of water. Once she had control of her stomach, she interjected with the only useful idea her mind had come up with. "We should raid the house."

Garner smiled and Treegar felt her stomach flip for an entirely different but not unrelated reason. "That's a good idea, you and I can go..."

"No." Treegar cut him off, everyone startled at that and she steeled her reaction to hide her own discomfort, "I'll take Dr Nagi. She needs the experience."

Dr Nagi looked even more startled than Garner and since his mouth was hanging adorably ajar, that was quite the feat on her part. Treegar continued her explanation, hoping that she could lay out sufficient arguments before any of her companions had been able to formulate a rebuttal.

"This mission does not possess a high level of risk and would be an opportunity for her to further prove that she is capable of providing adequate back up should anything happen to either Garner or myself. The house has already been scouted, I do not believe there remains more than the one decaying infected we saw, neutralizing them and restocking should be as simple a mission as we are likely to encounter." She faced Dr Nagi and addressed her directly, "will you accompany me?"

The doctor was still recovering and it took her a moment to respond beyond a slight nod, "Oh, um… yes. Yes I will."

Treegar nodded, spared Garner a brief glance and then stood, "We should leave as soon as you are ready. I believe you all wished to begin our journey immediately, this mission should not delay us."

"Right, just, let me, uh, grab my spear." Dr Nagi jumped up and hurried to the tent.

Treegar went to the door, hefted her mostly empty bag and readied her own weapons, making sure that they were comfortably secure before turning to unblock the door. Garner approached while she worked. She ignored him, waiting for him to say exactly what he came to say without assistance from her.

"A little abrupt, but you're right, she needs the experience and this is as controlled a situation as we are likely to get. Jason could use the experience too but sending them out there together isn't the best idea." He paused, briefly touching her shoulder, "Thanks, for, um, trying."

She nodded, concealing her face inside her visor and not turning to look at him. She didn't deserve his thanks, this suggestion was less to do with getting Dr Nagi more experience and confidence than it was finding a few minutes away from him so that she could inure herself to that future. A future without him.

"I'm ready." Dr Nagi announced from behind. Garner's hand dropped from Treegars shoulder and she immediately missed its presence.

"Then let go." With that announcement she pulled open the door and exited the studio, instinctively giving the area around the door a thorough once over before pressing forward. She caught a glimpse of Garner from her right eye and turned away, forging into the bright morning.

She could feel Dr Nagi moving behind her striving to match her steps but not quite catching the rhythm. The rain storm had worn away the snow and polished off stones laid in a path. The ground surrounding the stones was sopping and one step removed from becoming a mud pit but the stones themselves allowed for adequate purchase.

The landscape was completely changed, the sky transformed from a low bleak gray into a vaulting brilliant blue. Without the neutralizing effect of the snow and the clouds, the world was suddenly vibrant with color. Even the mud took on a rich ochre tone. It was a little overwhelming.

Unfortunately, with her eyes adjusted to the bright sunshine, the shadows became deeper and more impenetrable. She squinted to keep her eyes from fully adjusting and scanned their surroundings with suspicion. The wind brushed past, finding weaknesses in her gear that she was long since familiar with and sipping at her heat through them. It also sent the short grasses, barren bushes, and evergreen trees swaying in an intricate dance. She watched for anomalies in that dance.

They ascended the stairs and took one final look around before stepping into the shadow of the house and allowing their eyes to adjust to that midway point. With all the ambient light, the interior appeared nearly as black as night. The windows allowed the reflected sunlight in but there were no separate sources of light inside.

Nothing moved within the areas she could make out but then Treegar didn't expect the infected to have traveled far. She eased the door open and gave Dr Nagi a quick nod before swinging it open. Cold air rushed past her and the rank odor of rot and decay permeated her mask. Treegar had to pause for a moment before moving forward, her nose and stomach revolting at the stench.

"Oh lord!" Dr Nagi gasped, "What is that?"

Treegar didn't dignify that with a response, though she agreed that the smell was somehow even worse than she remembered. She stepped inside and eased her way around the room toward where she could have a clear line of sight to where she had last seen the infected. As her eyes adjusted to the gloom she could see that the pantry door was still held ajar, presumably by the body of the infected though she was reluctant to rely on that until she was able to see the floor.

She rounded the kitchen island slowly, placing her steps with care and listening to the shuffling steps of Dr Nagi behind her. The desiccated hand lay limp on the tile, bone and sinew shining white and yellow beside the dark browns of rotten flesh.

"Oh!"

That was all it took to set the hand in motion, scratching and scrambling against the tile. Flesh and blood oozed out of it and scraped grotesque marks through their dried counterparts. Treegar sprang forward, cracking the arm with the butt of her spear and breaking the brittle arm bones before her revulsion had a chance to take hold.

Next she forced the door open further. The arm was dragged back by its swing. The infected body pressed against the door, twitching at irregular intervals, adding moments of both pressure and release as the door shoved against it. The skink of rot intensified. Treegar took shallow breaths through her mouth to limit the horrors her nose was forced to endure.

The door stuck and Treegar slammed her shoulder into it to force it wide enough for her to get through. There was squelch and a crunch that sent a wave of nausea through her entire body.

The remains of the infected oozed more than they twitched, white tendons and bone peaked out through the browns and blacks of rotting flesh. With a swift movement, Treegar slammed her spear head into what looked like the head. The body stopped twitching and settled down into a pile of decay. Treegar stepped back and watched to make sure it was truly immobilized.

"Is that it?" Dr. Nagi asked. Treegar glanced back at the woman, despite the tremor in her voice she held her spear at the ready, aimed to strike either at Treegar or at the now immobile infected body.

Treegar nodded, "All clear. Keep your eyes open though, they might have friends."

Dr. Nagi nodded then began frantically glancing about as though another one was simply waiting for that precise moment to attack. Treegar turned from her and looked past the corpse. Lining shelves were both the supplies she knew they needed and a secondary source for the terrible rotting smell. Under and around the infected were dozens of broken jars of home canned food. The shattered glass stained and overrun by rotting food and billowing piles of mold. If she wanted to get to what remained on the shelves, she would need to either move or go through that toxic mess.

Despite her boots being waterproof and resistant to the Xeno-1 acid, Treegar wasn't certain that the thick, sharp glass wouldn't puncture a hole. She wrinkled her nose and looked for something to shift the pile with. A red handled broom was propped up in the corner of the pantry, just far enough away that she couldn't stretch out her hand and reach it but close enough that she tried anyways. When that failed, she pulled her spear out of the infected.

She used the butt of her spear to bump the broom handle, jostling it against the wall so that it bounced back and fell forward, over the infected remains and into her waiting hand. Now armed with something she wouldn't need to bring or clean, she began using the bristled end to push the body, glass jars, and debris out of the way. It was wet and heavy and really didn't want to move. Chunks of glass stuck out between ribs and rotten food mingled with intestines. Puffs of spores rose as she disturbed piles of mold. She had to scrape the broom across the floor to move most of it and even then the juices flowed back into place behind her efforts.

She had to move slowly, shifting each section at least three times before the area would remain mostly clear and even then when she moved forward newly displaced material would fall and she was forced to turn around and fix it. Eventually she had a relatively clear path from the door to the unbroken shelves.

The room was deeper than she had first expected. While the shelves closest to the door had much of their contents now living on the floor, the deeper shelves were filled with jars, cans and boxes of all manner of food.

She swung her backpack to her front and opened it. They

couldn't possibly carry everything here so she began filling her bag with the dry pre-packaged goods with a relatively high nutritional value. They were light and wouldn't run the risk of botulism like the home canning and best of all didn't require a can opener or other tool to access. She filled her bag until she could barely force the zipper closed and then shuffled her way out. Juices had oozed back into the path but the threat of glass remained firmly out of the way.

"Give me your bag." She ordered Dr. Nagi who jumped a little at her voice. To her credit, she reacted by twitching her spear toward the sound but followed it up by rescanning the area for other threats. Only after rechecking the area did the doctor swing her bag off her back and hold it out to Treegar.

Treegar almost smiled. The doctor was better prepared to survive on her own than she'd given her credit for. While nervousness was still evident, it had been channeled toward keeping them safe just as it ought. She accepted the backpack, handing her own off to Dr. Nagi and then returning to the pantry.

There were still plenty of dry packaged goods so Treegar filled the doctor's bag with more of those. With a full bag, she picked her way back through the path, stepping lightly through the areas where liquid had oozed in to refill the space.

"Done." If her mental inventory was anything to go by they should have more than enough food to get them to their destination, even if it might be a bit monotonous.

She left the pantry door as it was and led the way out of the house. Her eyes had adjusted to the gloom of the pantry so looking out the windows into the bright sunlight made them ache and water. She looked away and kept her gaze just to the side of the windows, allowing them time to readjust. It took longer than she would have liked but she moved slowly and waited just in case there was something outside that a moment of blindness would allow an opening for.

Once she could look out the window without pain, Treegar opened the door and stepped out onto the deck. The sky remained a vibrant, cloudless blue and the surrounding area was beautifully enclosed in a circle of trees. Only the eerie silence denoting the wrongness of the scene. It was like a still life painting without the life.

Dr Nagi took her time following Treegar out of the building, allowing her eyes the same adjustment period. When she did, they met each other's eyes and then set out down the path back to the studio.

12

Fear. The virus hated that emotion. So basic in all the minds it inhabited. So important to their survival. Their old fears had been erased, replaced with Its own. Death, fire, and the unknown memory that It somehow knew spoke of the future.

*   *   *

Traveling in the mid morning sunshine was so brilliant and beautiful it almost lulled Jason into a false sense of security. Lucky for him his gear, his companions, and the distinct absence of animal noise kept his mind focused. When there had been snow or rain the lack of birdsong had seemed normal and natural, now in the sunshine it felt wrong. This wasn't a stroll on a sunny day. It was a trek through dangerous enemy territory.

About an hour into their journey they intersected with a road. This one was also clogged with abandoned cars, several of which crashed into each other and some which had been caught in a bomb crater. There didn't appear to be any infected roaming along it so Garner led them across. They crouched and kept their bodies low, ducking between cars wherever possible.

Jason followed behind Jaspreet and attempted to copy Garner's movements. The crouching made his knee ache and he had to alter his walking to compensate. It made him slow, the gap between him and Jaspreet widening with every step, but thankfully Treegar made no effort to hurry him. She remained solidly behind him, protecting the rear of their little group.

He saw Garner flinch back after the fourth car. A moment later Garner was slamming his spear and a soft crunch carried through the too silent air. He stepped lightly forward and both he and Jaspreet disappeared around the curve of the vehicle.

When Jason reached that spot he saw the body of an infected, bloated and rotting, no longer active as its brains spilled gray-pink onto the pavement. He hurried to catch up and leave that gruesome mess behind.

Once they were off the road and back into the woods, everyone straightened up, taking a moment to stretch and reorient themselves. Jason caught up with Jaspreet, "Hey, when you were on the computer, did you check out any research forums?"

She gave him a bemused look, "I did, though probably not the same ones you did. I saw the post you made about the meteorite, though."

Jason considered following that line and finding out her thoughts but figured if she had something to say or add she would say it regardless of his questioning. "Yeah, what other stuff did you read?"

Jaspreet looked away and began scanning the area. Jason took his cue from her, turning his head to watch the scenery as they walked. "Apparently it has been confirmed that Xeno-1 is extraterrestrial in origin. But then we already knew that. Several groups online have been debating if this was an accident of the universe or a deliberate attack by a hostile, intelligent alien species. Within that last group there are several sub groups, some of which think Xeno-1 was sent to aid in communication, others think it was sent to wipe us out–by the way I'm personally of that opinion, and then a third group who think it is an unfortunate byproduct of first contact overtures. I went down a bit of a rabbit hole there. How about you?"

"Sounds like your colleagues haven't made much progress."

Jaspreet hummed her agreement, "most of them are too used

to working in theory to make the shift to the current practical problem.”

“Well, a group in Sweden thinks they can communicate with Xeno-1. Oh, and some people in Milan seem to have found an on/off switch in Xeno-1’s DNA.”

“What?” Jaspreet spoke over him, she had turned from her scanning to look him dead in the eye, or visor since the bright sunlight made it hard to see each other's faces.

“They’ve only triggered it in lab settings so far.” He hastily qualified and immediately wished he had better news as her shoulders slumped and she turned back to her duties.

“Oh,” her tone was dismissive.

“But it has potential. They’re isolating the radiation bands which trigger it and hope to get it out of the lab and in a more portable form. It’s still early days but it's something.”

“I guess.”

They walked in silence for several steps before she spoke up again. “I just don’t think anyone is considering what comes after.”

“After?”

“After, after we either stop it, contain it, or die from it. Ecosystems aren’t just plants and bugs. They aren’t designed to work that way. Even if we stop Xeno-1 in its tracks today, turned it all off so to speak, we are facing an environmental collapse on par with the ice age. And who knows what that is even going to look like?”

Jason gasped, glancing around at all the trees, ferns, and grasses. He gave a moment to think about how many of those relied on birds and rodents to spread their seeds? How many required pruning and care from those same creatures? “What are we going to do?"

"I have no idea." Jaspreet sighed. "After this, after your mission, I'm going home. There might not be anything to return to, no one answered my messages, but I'd rather try than not."

Jason looked at her, her solid stance, even pace, and constantly moving head. She was in so many ways a duplicate of Garner and Treegar now. "Are you sure?"

She nodded, "Yes, I need to know. Even if I die trying, it will be worth it."

Her tone filled Jason with sympathetic sadness. He might have nothing and no one to return to, the mission for Agatha being the only thing that kept him moving, but Jaspreet was different. She had friends and family, she was a lovely, humane, and social person. At the base she had been the one to force him out of his shell. Her team had functioned as a family far more than this own had. It had taken him ages to even learn the names of his staff while she'd known the names and familial situations of all her staff within a week of meeting them. He could only imagine how making such connections would hurt when they were severed. He'd been too wrapped up in his own grief to even consider her pain.

"I never asked, are you okay?" He hesitated, stumbling over the imprecision of his words, "I mean, with this trip, being forced out of the base, leaving..."

She huffed a small laugh, "a little late for that check in, but better late than not at all. I'm fine. It hurt," she paused and Jason left the silence for her to fill in her own time and with her own words, "it hurt that no one spoke up for us. Well, no one who didn't come along." She looked behind her at Treegar and then continued, "I always think that people will choose strength over weakness. And this crisis has proven that that is sometimes true. But I was mostly wrong. People are inherently weak and selfish. They are afraid of what they don't understand and will sacrifice everything and everyone they deem either a threat or not part of their little group. I wish we were better than that, but we aren't. Maybe earth would be better without us. Wipe us all out and start over. I'm not sure all the animals were caught and Xeno-1 hasn't spread everywhere yet. Maybe the ecological gaps can be filled before they cascade." She finished with a shrug, "maybe."

Jason had no idea how to respond to that. While he'd spent most of his life seeing humans, including himself, as selfish and self-centered, he didn't like hearing that from Jaspreet, one of the few people he'd met who didn't fall into that category. Agatha had been like that too. Selfless even in the face of her great pain, reaching out to lift others rather than seeking to push them down or control them.

He hadn't expected this level of fatalism and defeat from Jaspreet. At the base she'd been a beacon of hope and humanity. He struggled to accept that he'd somehow missed this shift inside of her. But then again, they'd been traveling for weeks and he had only just asked her how she was doing, he certainly fell into the selfish and self-centered category. He dropped back and let her move ahead on her own, uncertain of how he could possibly comfort her.

*   *   *

The remainder of the day Jason worked through his own thoughts. He pushed aside his uncertainty regarding Jaspreet's disappointment in humanity back to the research she had shared with him. If Xeno-1 was sent by aliens, who engineered it with a genetic on/off switch, how would those hypothetical aliens activate that switch on a global scale? They could do it from orbit, maybe. Or send down another meteorite or probe or even a bunch of probes to do it. Or, they could use the original meteorite. That seemed like the most efficient method and they knew the meteorite had a strong continuing connection to Xeno-1 at least up until they had broken it.

Jason paused in his stride for a moment before simple momentum propelled him back into step. What if in breaking the lattice, they had destroyed the only method of turning Xeno-1 off?

Would putting the lattice back together fix it? Was he even capable of fixing it? He could try, it might be nothing, based entirely on half baked theories and very little substance, but it was something he could do, something he could control.

When they set up camp that night, in the woods but not far from the road they had loosely been following, he dug the lattice fragments from where they had settled at the bottom of his bag. There was still sufficient natural light for the strange metal to glimmer with opalescence. He experimented fitting the largest pieces together, they didn't connect. He pulled out more pieces and twisted the fragments this way and that trying to find a match.

"What are you doing?" Jaspreet shuffled up to him and watched as he struggled to fit together two connection points.

"Following up on a theory. Remember how I told you about the possible on/off switch?"

He caught her nod from the corner of his eye.

"Well, if Xeno-1 was created by aliens, and they designed it with this on/off switch, it makes sense to me that they would have sent down something to activate that switch." He looked up from the pieces in his hands and gauged her reaction.

She nodded slowly and pursed her lips, "I'm not sure I agree with your logic, but are you suggesting that the meteorite might have been the key to turning Xeno-1 off after all?"

"Yes!" Jason exclaimed, "and maybe it still could be. Now I know we don't have all of the other materials that were surrounding the lattice, and the lattice is broken, but maybe we could put it back together and with all the records of what you removed, we could possibly recreate the original structure of the meteorite."

At that she shook her head, "No, we couldn't." She paused and Jason felt his momentary hope begin to sink. "And I'm not sure it would even be necessary. Any species sufficiently advanced not only to make it from their planet to ours but to design Xeno-1 and a way to turn it off, wouldn't have trusted on chance to get their technology down here. They encased the lattice with materials designed to absorb the heat and impact of atmospheric entry. By my calculations the meteorite lost approximately half of its original mass in our atmosphere." She took a long breath and continued, " If your theory regarding the original purpose of the meteorite is correct, then I'm certain that it applies primarily to the lattice and not the rest of the meteorite."

Jason looked at the separate pieces in his hands, " that's good to know. Unfortunately I was kind of hoping we could use the other materials to hold the structure back together. Besides that, I suck at puzzles."

Jaspreet huffed a laugh at that last bit which made Jason smile to himself. "Well, I have something to hold the pieces together, it's not perfect but it should help them hold their shape until we figure out something else." She pulled her bag over and opened a side pocket. The zipper stuck twice due to how overful the main compartment was and how the fabric had distorted, but once it was open she had what she was looking for in half a second at most. Superglue and a roll of tape.

Jason grinned, "you take those from the studio?"

Jaspreet shrugged, "I don't think their former owner is going to need them. Now, let's get working on this puzzle and see what we can manage together." Jaspreet gave him a hopeful smile and he thought he saw a tiny bit of her earlier cynicism melt away.

13

It dug within itself and found a link, a link that went beyond the disparate fragments of Itself. It was anchored deeply into the oldest parts, remaining so steadfast that the virus instinctively knew that to root it out would be the same as killing itself. It had found its doom and was powerless to remove it.

*　　*　　*

Treegar had successfully and cowardly managed to avoid talking with Garner for the past day and a half. Other than a quick download regarding the successful supply run with Dr. Nagi she hadn't spoken to him . She wasn't sure if he'd noticed her avoidance and didn't want to think about her motivations for avoiding him.

The day was gray with thin high cloud cover that left the sky looking more like a white dome than a collection of cumulous, stratus, and nimbus cloud formations. She couldn't remember enough about the different types of clouds to differentiate between them, all she knew was that today, they looked like one big blanket really high in the sky.

Regardless of the cloud cover, the day was dry and that was what really mattered. They made good time yesterday despite the deep shadows occasionally playing tricks on them and today looked to be just as productive. That didn't bring the satisfaction it should have. She liked making good time, it usually gave her a sense of satisfaction. Something felt different about that now.

While she focused on her surroundings, Garner picked up his pace and came up beside her. Treegar considered dropping back or speeding up to avoid walking side by side with him but her stupid heart had missed him and the logical part of her brain knew that she should savor these last days with him.

"So, what's wrong?" He opened the conversation with a cudgel.

"Nothing." The answer came reflexively and too fast, sounding just as childish and defensive as she knew it to be. She let out a sigh and tried again, "there's nothing wrong. We are making good time. If the weather holds and we don't get lost we should be there in a few days."

"You know what I mean. What's wrong with us? Why are you mad at me?" He didn't reach out to touch her, didn't even try to catch her eyes, just walked beside her and scanned their surroundings.

She felt her resistance falter and her shoulders slumped. Treegar remained on watch, walking and carrying her spear at the ready, but allowed the softer parts of herself to guide this conversation. "You're going to leave me." She mumbled.

"What?" Garner stumbled but quickly righted himself and performed a brief half-jog to catch back up. "I'm not leaving you."

"You won't have a choice. We both know I'm not fit to pass any psych evals so I'll be kicked out after we get back. You're basically perfect, though I have no idea how after all the crap we've seen, so they are going to keep you. So, I'll be out on my butt and you'll keep serving what's left of our country." She shrugged at the end as though pretending that it didn't matter could make it so.

Garner made a noise as though he wanted to argue but then fell silent again. They moved along like that for several minutes, the only sounds coming from the scuff of their boots and the murmur of the doctors behind them.

"I hadn't thought about it like that. You sure you won't pass an eval?" He added, even though the resignation in his tone said that he knew the answer.

Despite knowing that he knew the answer, she indulged him by answering, "the thought of undressing for a physical makes me literally break out into a cold sweat. I've been wearing muddy, dirty clothing for the past several days because the thought of taking them off even to just shake them out makes me feel like my heart is about to explode. I don't know if I could manage to take a shower without having a panic attack. You know as well as I do that my mind is doing some crazy acrobatics to get me through all of this. After everything we've seen, after everything I've done, I'm not healthy and I probably won't be for a very, very long time. If ever."

They traveled in silence for a long time, their path taking them up another incline. Madison allowed herself to revel in the simple fact of his presence. It was comforting like her face shield, a gentle barrier that was at once a part of her and a part from her. He protected her, just like the rest of her gear. She hated the thought of being without him.

"Who am I talking to right now?" Garner murmured.

Madison startled out of her thoughts and there was a moment where both she and Treegar wanted to answer. Finally, she settled on, "Me. Treegar is keeping us safe and walking, Madison is telling you how she feels." It was the most distinct she had yet managed to articulate. For the past several months she had primarily been Treegar, with Madison cowering in the back of her mind to avoid all the cold, fear, and monotonous horror. But something about their time in the studio, the waiting and knowing that the end was near, had allowed them to interact. She was two halves of a whole but she wasn't really whole.

"That sounds like a difficult balance."

"It is. It's new." She admitted. Sometimes it felt like balancing on top of a monkey bar, unstable and unsustainable. Other times it felt like her natural state, like she was almost who she had once been.

"I hope it works out. I like talking to all of you. I like all of you." He huffed, "and you have a point, even if the military takes you back they are unlikely to station us together again. Though, to be honest, I'm not as sure about them taking me back as you seem to be."

They went a few more steps, absorbing that statement. The air had warmed through the day and for the first time in months the air gaps in her gear weren't sucking away heat. She could feel warmth building around her body and imagined cooking inside this suit during the heat of summer. It sounded dreadful. Maybe there was a chance she could take it off, maybe she could be safe, feel safe, without it?

"What if we didn't go back?"

The question broke through the silence and opened a floodgate of possibility. "But, you said..." she trailed off.

"I know. We have an obligation to fulfill but as you rightly pointed out, that would involve us being separated. Not to mention how are we supposed to find our way to anything remotely resembling an actual command structure. We could just stay together. I don't know what Jason wants to do after this but I'm sure Jaspreet would like to go home. That at least gets us on Vancouver Island, there has to be fewer infected there, we should be safer. After that, you and I, well maybe we could find a place and settle down. Work through everything that's happened to us. I can get to know Treegar and Madison better or you can work on reintegrating those parts of yourself. And you can get to know me, Vincent, not just Garner."

She was speechless. Both Madison and Treegar, completely bowled over but that speech. It was more than she could have hoped for.

"What do you think?" Garner asked shyly after she hadn't answered for several paces.

Treegar took over as Madison had become a whirling dervish of confusion. "That sounds excellent. We would be honored to accompany you and Dr. Nagi to the island. As for everything after that, that also sounds ideal. Thank you."

Garner chuckled, "I think I caught that, that was Treegar." He kicked a small rock and followed its path with his eyes.

Treegar looked away and resumed scanning the area for threats leaving Madison to pull herself together and respond, "it was!"

He chuckled again, "Hi Madison."

"Hi!" Madison laughingly replied and kicked a small rock of her own. This was good, they had a plan, they had a future. Suddenly she was almost eager to reach the sisters home and begin the next phase of their journey. Treegar squashed any foolishness but that didn't stop Madison from mentally jumping up and down in celebration.

*   *   *

As they moved further west they encountered more homes and settlements. With that level of urbanization came more human infected. By mid morning on the third day they had already snuck around two different clusters of infected. It was odd, none of the infected they saw were animals, they were all humans, often wearing the remains of rain coats, boots, and other plastic clothing.

Treegar began triple checking her gear and performing visual inspections of her companions. She may not know how exactly Xeno-1 got through those other peoples protective clothing but she could do her best to protect her companions.

After skirting around the edges of a small town beside a lake, they were forced into a valley. The road which seemed the easiest passage through it was periodically clogged with crashed or abandoned cars. As the sun set they came upon an abandoned minivan blocked on its way into the valley by a tangle of cars. There was enough space around it that Treegar was sure they could back it up and get it turned around.

"We should take this, even if it only gets us a little further it will provide better protection for the night than the tent." She began testing the handles, hoping that one of them would be unlocked. The passenger side was locked tight but when she rounded the drivers side she saw that the drivers door wasn't properly closed. It hung open a half inch as though whoever exited it hadn't managed to close it behind them. She eased the door open. The hinges groaned in protest, water that had been trapped in the door seam spilled out and splashed on the pavement.

The air inside the van was damp and heavy with the scent of mildew. It was otherwise clear with no hint of rotting flesh. There was even a set of keys fallen into the footwell. "Looks like we're in luck." She called out, scooping up the keys and putting the one that looked most right into the ignition. The van sputtered to life with reluctance. The electronics sprang on and she pressed the button to unlock the remaining doors. "Let's go." The engine sputtered, "sounds like this guy doesn't have much left in him."

The gas tank was sitting just above the red line but that was better than she had hoped for so she had no complaints. Sleeping in this van would be significantly safer than their tent and would mean that she and Garner could actually sleep through the night.

Garner and the doctors piled in, with Garner taking shotgun and the doctors sitting in the row behind. Once their doors were closed she cranked the wheels and turned the van so it was now going up the hill and away from the valley. The hill was long and winding. The sun dipped behind the mountain and twilight shifted suddenly into night. The headlights kept the road ahead lit but that pool of light was all she had to guide them by.

Suddenly a figure loomed in the distance, shambling along the road. Treegar turned the wheel to avoid the infected but it lunged toward them at the last second, glancing off the right side of the van. The side mirror came off and the infected was thrown off into the darkness. She kept her foot on the gas and pushed forward. The road began to level out but she kept her foot down, finally managing to pick up a little speed. The speedometer hit 50 km/h then 55.

The engine sputtered. It coughed. Momentum kept them rolling forward. She worked to draw as much from the vehicle as she could. The road dipped, giving them a gravity fed burst of speed. She pumped the gas, seeking the final drops of combustion.

They crested a little hill and then tipped forward and down a long downhill slope. She took her foot off the gas, allowing gravity to power their descent for as long as it could. The engine coughed again. It sputtered and then died. The wheels kept turning and the electronics remained lit but the engine was quite literally out of gas. She navigated their descent as the hill leveled out. The van slowed and then finally hit an incline and stopped completely. She threw the brakes on, engaging the emergency brake just as the van considered rolling backward and completely stopped their movement.

"End of the line." Garner observed.

"Better than nothing." Jaspreet agreed, "Great driving, where'd you learn to drive like that?"

Treegar just shrugged, "I'm locking the doors before our battery dies too. You should all consider getting a little shut eye."

After everyone murmured their assent, Treegar locked the doors and turned the van off.

*   *   *

Daylight came late between the mountains with the sky overhead already a lightening gray by the time the sun began to outline the mountains with its light. Treegar was one of the first to wake, watching the sky shift through the morning range of colors before settling into the usual wintry clouds, though they were significantly closer than they had been the day before.

Raindrops splashed against the windshield and she watched as they gathered together to form rivulets until the glass was so saturated that it was impossible to discern anything beyond the ripples of the drops as they landed.

She looked at their surroundings. It was a green, wooded mountainside. The road slicing a path through the mountains along with what appeared to be a natural break. She turned to the right and allowed her eyes to linger on Garner's sleeping form. What would it be like to live in relative safety with him? To feel his touch, not through gear, but on her skin? The thought was at once exciting and terrifying. She forced her observations back to their surroundings.

To the right, up the hill several meters was another vehicle, crashed into the barrier and long since abandoned. Tree debris littered it and even from the distance she could see rust eating away at the crumpled parts. An idea struck her but she sat on it until she heard her companions begin to stir.

"Mhrff..." Garner groaned as he attempted to roll over but discovered that he couldn't. "Mmmm?" Madison watched as his eyes fluttered open and met hers. Even with the additional shadowing of the visor she could make out the soft smile that lit his face upon seeing her. "Hey." The greeting was more breath than anything else and she wished she could feel it caress her skin.

"Hey yourself, I've got an idea." She launched right in, knowing that he might need a moment to fully wake up but eager to move forward. "See that car over there?" She pointed so he would have an easier time finding it but he still struggled for a moment either due to the fogginess of sleep or his eyes adjusting.

"Yeah," he blinked several times but kept his eyes on the vehicle, "doesn't exactly look drivable."

"I'm not thinking about driving it. Unlike this beauty, it was abandoned because it was no longer drivable. I bet it still has gas in it. I don't know about the rest of you, but I'd prefer driving through these mountains to walking them."

"Gas? Yeah, you're right." He pulled himself up and took another look at the wrecked car, "but how do we get it?"

She shrugged, "Have you ever siphoned gas before?" It was a long shot but once again, her checkered past might come in handy.

"No, can't say that I have." He paused and his skin went a little pale, "that's where you suck it into your mouth or something, right?"

Treegar shook her head, "No, you really shouldn't try doing that. It's where you blow air into the tank through one tube, creating pressure inside it and then allowing it to flow out a second tube. If we can find some tubes, we should be able to manage that."

"Right, that makes sense. Then let's find some tubes. And I guess something to put the gas in since I doubt this van is getting over there without at least a little top up."

"Yup, let's wake the nerds and see what they have to say."

*　　*　　*

Once everyone was awake Treegar finally discovered the benefits of actually discussing her plans with the group rather than just telling them to do what she thought was best.

"We could pull the drainage plug and catch the gas as it comes out. That only requires something to catch the gas, no tubing needed." Dr. Nagi suggested, looking upsettingly like this was the most obvious solution and why hadn't Treegar or Garner thought of it.

"The what?" Garner asked, unashamed to display his lack of automotive knowledge.

"The drainage plug. A lot of cars have them. Might depend on the model. I had to do it once when I was in grad school. It wasn't hard, just a little smelly and messy."

Treegar nodded, "let's make that plan A. If we find a hose then siphoning can be our back up."

They searched the van and found a red and white cooler as well as several empty water bottles. There was a tool kit with socket wrenches and screwdrivers as well as a fuzzy blanket and various other sundries. They collected everything that looked useful and exited the van. The road ahead of them was steep and getting up the short distance between vehicles had Treegar grateful that, if her plan worked, they wouldn't need to hike up the whole thing.

The passenger side window had been broken in the crash, so Treegar used her elbow to break more of the glass. With that obstacle dealt with, she reached inside and opened the door. It stuck a little but gave after a firm tug. The interior was littered with wet and rotting garbage. She wrinkled her nose and leaned inside to unlock the other doors. Garner stood watch while the rest of them sifted through the detritus, pulling out empty drink cups and pop bottles.

Once they had gathered all that the car had to offer, Dr Nagi offered to go under the car and be the one to open the drainage plug. "It makes sense, I at least know what I'm looking for." She pulled the tool kit under with her and wriggled her way deeper under the belly of the vehicle.

More and more of her disappeared under the cars belly, the heels of her boots pressing into the ground to push her deeper. "Found it." She called out, "pass me a bottle."

Garner did as she said and held a bottle as deep as he could under the car, near where he thought her hand should be able to reach it. He pulled back without the bottle a moment later.

"No good," the bottle came rolling out onto the gravel and flattened grass, "too tall. You'll need to cut the top off."

Treegar handed Garner one of the empty fast food cups, "give this a shot, I'll take care of the bottle." She hurried after the bottle as it rolled and bounced down the hill. She had to take long thudding strides to reach it and even then she only stopped its progress by placing her steps in front of it. It bounced off her foot and jumped to the side. She scooped down and grabbed it only then looking up to see how far down the hill she had traveled. She was half again as far down the hill as the van was. It was a long hike back up and she cursed the bottle every step of the way.

When she arrived back at the car Dr Scortdato and Garner were trading off passing Dr Nagi drinking cups and then emptying them into the cooler. The cooler had an inch or so at the bottom but the system seemed to be working. Treegar opened the offending pop bottle, dunked it into the gasoline and forced as much of the liquid into it as she could before pulling it out and screwing on the top.

The four of them worked continuously until all the bottles were full and then Treegar took it upon herself to carry them down to the van.

She placed the bottles on the floor of the driver's seat and then popped the gas tank open. The bottles remained there while she moved to the back of the van and unscrewed the gas cap. She then grabbed the bottles, two at a time and poured their contents into the tank. It took a very short period of time for them all to empty and then she was trekking back up the hill for more. She stank of fuel and she could feel the strain of all the trips up and down in the muscles just above her knees.

The little cooler was half full when she arrived which made filling bottles much easier but before she had the third one full Dr Nagi was wriggling her way out from under the car.

"That's the last of it." She announced.

Treegar nodded and tried to calculate how much gas that worked out to. Eight bottles plus what was left in the cooler. The group trudged back down the hill carting the last of their spoils. She had left the gas cap off so pouring the gas in took hardly a minute. Getting it to pour nicely from the cooler took a bit longer but they used the drink cups as intermediaries and that seemed to get the task done with a minimum of loss. Finally it was done.

They all reeked of gasoline but it would all be worth it if the van could get them a little further on their journey. They shoved the bottles into the cooler and shut the lid on them before throwing them all into the very back of the van.

Treegar tried to start the van again. It sparked but the engine didn't turn over. She tried again. And again but this time she pressed on the gas pedal while turning the key. The engine roared to life and revved high. That was all it took to have her leaping to put the van into drive and get them out of there.

14

The virus was angry and afraid. Angry in response to the fear. Angry that it could not stop the fear. Angry at what the fear meant. It absorbed minds, more lives, more beings into itself. It stole from their minds, searching for a reason, an explanation which would take the power away from the fear. It soon found that the answer lay not in their minds but in the trail of fear parts of it had encountered. A group which defied infection by triggering the most primal fear within the virus itself.

*   *   *

It was impossible to know when the doctor and his companions would arrive, which left Charissa and Penelope on edge all the time. They picked away at the infected. They cleaned up what they could from *the day* and they moved the bodies in the basement so they were piled in the furthest corner, away from where Sophia and Atticus might happen upon them. And they spent time with the kids. They even did some baking, the smell of fresh baked bread and cookies combating the pervasive odor of death and decay.

It wasn't much but it kept them busy and, at least for Charissa, it kept her from spiraling. As the days passed she became more; comfortable wasn't the right word, maybe more accepting, yes; she became more accepting of what she had done. Honestly, when she looked rationally at the situation she had killed long before those people attacked. The infected might be dead, or they might not be. She had no idea if a cure could be found which could bring back those infected with Xeno-1. That begged the question, if they were savable, was killing them the same as killing uninfected people? She had shoved her spear through the heads of far more infected than the handful of uninfected people she had killed in the house.

Knowing that it was defense helped. Looking at Sophia and Atticus reminded her that any moral grounds for nonviolence were meaningless compared to their safety. She would bathe in blood if it kept those angels safe.

The days had blurred together for her but by Penelope's count it had been a week since Timothy died. With no way to bury him, they had settled on a ceremony to honor him instead.

While Penelope prepared for the ceremony, Charissa did the rounds. There weren't many spots where the infected could get close enough to the house for her to reach them with her spear. If it wouldn't draw more of them, she would have used their remaining bullets on them, but that would only make the situation worse.

"We're ready." Penelope announced from the hall, her voice carrying through the main floor of the house.

Charissa closed the window she had been working out of and moved out of the room and down the hallway to where Timothy was laid out. Sophia and Atticus were already kneeling next to their father. Penelope had surrounded him with flowers made out of folded and twisted crepe paper and the whole room was heavy with essential oils. It was a vast improvement over the general stink of decay the whole house had taken on and yet it felt false. Covering up the smell of him rotting didn't make him any less dead.

Penelope knelt with her children, beside Atticus, and waited for Charissa to sit next to Sophia before beginning. "Timothy, you were the best of men. You were unfailingly good and kind to each and everyone you met. You once told me that your secret was simple, that you knew that everyone was just as complete an individual as you were and you treated them like it. You never saw that as special." Penelope choked up and her voice came out thick and strained. Atticus leaned over, his head pressing into her arm. Penelope reached around and pulled him into her side. "I love you so much. We love you so much. You may never know just how much we miss you but I am so grateful that we had you while we did."

She cleared her throat and continued, "you were brave and strong, always thinking ahead. You kept us safe and provided for even during impossible times. You are the reason we have survived this long. Tim, I don't know how we are going to make it without you." She swallowed and then pulled her eyes from Timothy's face and looked down at her kids, "we are doing our best. We won't let you be forgotten." She paused and then asked, "would either of you like to say something to your daddy?"

Charissa watched her niece and nephew look from their mom to their dead father, the thoughts in their heads written clearly on their faces. Sophia opened her mouth and then closed it. Atticus opened his and then looked at his sister and reconsidered.

"I'm sorry." Sophia whispered, her mouth barely moving. Tears welled up in her eyes and she bent forward, her body crushing the paper flowers as she pressed her forehead onto her fathers stomach. "I'm so sorry daddy." She continued to mumble into his chest but the words were lost, only the sag of her shoulders and the shaking of her tiny frame hinted at their content.

Penelope leaned over, reaching out to her daughter and drawing her unresisting into a hug. Atticus disappeared between them, crushed into the familial hug.

All Charissa could do was watch this small broken family mourn. Words pressed at her mind, pushing their way up her throat until she had to speak. Heavy truths forcing their way out of her lips. "I'm sorry I got you killed. It's my fault. I shouldn't have done what I did. I should have died, not you." The words fell like toads, slimy and unpleasant but real. Her chin trembled and she felt her jaw clench but the words continued to fall, unable to be stopped now that she had begun. "It's my fault. I'm so sorry." They fell over and over again until words failed and tears took their place.

"It's not." Sophia's voice broke through her sobs. Charissa pulled her sorrow tight to her chest and looked up. Unnoticed by her, Penelope, Atticus, and Sophia had sat up and turned to her. Their faces were masks of confusion, pity, and sorrow which made Charissa want to run out of the house without her protective gear. "It's not your fault." Sophia clarified, "It's mine. I got daddy killed."

Charissa shook her head vehemently, "no, no you didn't."

The little girl countered by vigorously nodding her head, "yes I did."

"Honey," Penelope broke the argument before either side could dig in their heels. "Why do you feel that way?"

Her daughter looked up at her mom and then quickly back down, fidgeting with her fingers. "Because, if I hadn't let that man grab me, or if I'd been able to slippery fish him, then he couldn't have used me to threaten daddy. Then daddy could have stopped him without getting hurt, and then daddy would still be here."

"Hmmm…"

Charissa felt at a loss for words so she looked at Penelope for answers.

"And how would you have stopped the man from grabbing you?"

Sophia shrugged, "dunno, been faster I guess."

"Okay. How would you have slippery fished your way out of it? As I remember, you tried but he had a good hold on you and you couldn't get out."

Again she shrugged.

"Alright, say you didn't get grabbed, or that you had been able to escape. What makes you think the man wouldn't have still shot daddy? He had a gun, remember, and your daddy didn't."

"He coulda fought him," Sophia asserted.

"And probably still been shot. It wasn't your fault." Sophia shook her head.

"It wasn't your fault." Charissa echoed her sister's statement, watching as the words bounced off Sophia's emotional shell.

"Nor was it yours." Penelope followed up, staring Charissa down. "You couldn't have stopped him any faster than you did. You did your best and you protected the rest of us. He would have killed us all, either with bullets or starvation, that was their plan. None of us are responsible for the actions of other people. We are never responsible for what other people choose, right?" She spoke so clearly and firmly that despite her self recriminations Charissa was forced to see the sense in what Penelope was saying.

When no one responded, Penelope gave her daughter's shoulder a gentle shake, "right?"

"Right." Came the soft reply and Charissa felt her own mouth breath out her agreement.

"Good, so to recap, we are not responsible for other people's choices, right?" Everyone, even Atticus, nodded in agreement.

"And that means that what happened to daddy wasn't any of our faults, right?" Charissa drew in a long breath, pulling the heavy scents of mingled essential oils into her lungs and then nodded in agreement. Penelope was right, she wasn't responsible for what those people did. Maybe if she'd moved faster, or distracted the man in some other way, but thinking like that would only drive her crazy and would do nothing to bring Timothy back or protect the kids in the future.

She looked at the sagging serenity of Timothy's face and felt a particle of guilt lift.

15

Frbulanu nuzzled xer oldest youngling. Just out of the pouch and already eagerly socializing and absorbing knowledge. The little would only tolerate xer parental smothering for a moment before bounding away to look at a console and pepper the operator with questions. The operator, Kafdal, answered the questions with amusement and patience, two things that were practical requirements for colonization missions such as this.

An alert chimed from the panel beside xer right paw. With a few clicks of xer claws xe accepted the computers trajectory and confirmed launch on the next phase of planetary preparation. The ship shuddered for a moment as the containment unit released and stabilization boosters compensated for the shift in mass.

Xer child hopped back to xer and chittered a question. Frbulanu hummed an explanation, explaining how the capsule would continue the ecological reformation of the planet to better suit their dietary needs and to refill any ecological holes. Xe then began quizzing xer youngling on the species of their home world. They were eager to show off their new knowledge and bounded around the bridge declaring facts about the various creatures of their past, ones which might soon be finding ground in their new home.

*　　　*　　　*

Jaspreet had undersold her enthusiasm for puzzles. Traveling in the van allowed them time to lay out and piece together the largest pieces of the lattice. She'd managed to find where they fit together and when a perfect connection was made, they learned a fascinating new thing about the lattice, the sections automatically refused together. The expected need for tape and superglue to stick the pieces back together was no longer necessary. Jason wondered just how many of the fragments at the bottom of his bag had already fused back together just by virtue of accidentally bumping into one another. It definitely helped them verify when a correct connection was made, though even without that verification Jason could tell that Jaspreet was exponentially better at this task than he was.

"It helps that I spent weeks staring at the blasted thing." She joked when he would remark on her progress. To him each section looked much like the others, but somehow she could make out the details that made each section different. He could admit that he was more useful holding the pieces for her to pick through than trying to place them himself.

Treegar steered them around piles of debris and abandoned vehicles, frequently swerving from one side of the road to the other and using the shoulders to go around obstacles. The light increased, which seemed to speed up both their work on the lattice and Treegars navigation.

The road grew more and more clogged with crashed and abandoned vehicles as well as several large branches. They managed to scrape through despite that sometimes being a very literal description of how tight the paths were.

Unfortunately, after about an hour, their luck ran out. The bridge before them was packed with smashed cars, a semi jackknifed across several lanes, and dozens of cars abandoned to either side of the accidents. Jason took a moment to mentally assess where all of those people had gone. He really hoped they weren't roaming around still and that time would at least grant them rest.

"This is it." Treegar announced, redundantly since she had

already shut the car off.

"How close did we get?" Jason asked, he'd been too distracted by the lattice to read the signs they'd passed.

"No idea. Somewhere past a place called Mission. We're on the BC-7, we'll need to check a map or something, or keep going until there's a good sign." Her tone was less brusque than normal, almost soft, though Jason would never characterize Treegar as actually soft in any manner.

"Right, better pack up then." He looked to Jaspreet who was holding a smallish piece onto the reconstructed lattice structure and wiggling it to see if the connection would fuse and thereby confirm her decision. When her lips curved into a rueful smile, Jason knew that the material had once again done its strange alchemy. She released the piece and held the section out to him.

"Okay, be careful. We have no idea if the refused sections are as stable as the rest of the structure. I don't relish redoing all of that work a second time." She handed the partially reconstructed lattice to Jason.

The structure was really taking shape. The breaks where it had shattered under the pressure of the hydraulic press completely disappeared due to its mysterious refusing ability. He put the remaining pieces inside the structure to make sure all of it fit inside the bag.

"Ready." He declared and then he and Jaspreet joined the soldiers outside of the van.

The bridge sat low over a swollen river. They made their way down its length, slipping between vehicles and watching for infected. Jason noted that the side barrier was broken in several places, with only most of those spots filled by vehicles teetering precariously on the edge. Debris caught on windshields and piled up against tires, blown about by the icy wind off the river.

It didn't take them long to cross the bridge but the piled up traffic didn't end with that choke point.

The land around them was a strong contrast to the mountains they had started the day's journey in. It was flat and brown, the only trees were stark skeletons reaching out into the gray sky. Short buildings only added to the overall flat nature of the surroundings. Evergreens stood in the distance, creating a border before low mountains rose to meet the hanging clouds.

Train tracks parallel the road and the group moved off the pavement onto the tracks. The gravel between the rails crunched softly under their boots. They passed an intersection naming the road they were traveling along as the Lougheed Highway, not that that meant anything to any of them.

Finally they reached a green road sign that read:

Port Coquitlam 27

Vancouver 55

"Well, that doesn't seem too far. Think we can make it tonight?" Garner asked the group.

Jason bounced on the balls of his feet, feeling a slight twinge in his knee as he did. They could make it tonight. The sun was still climbing the sky. All that driving had shaved at least a day of walking off their trip. They might spend tonight at the sisters house!

"Maybe." Treegar replied, "but didn't they say that they were surrounded by infected? I don't know if tackling that after a day of walking is a good idea. It would be better to get close and then hunker down for the night. Tackle that problem in the morning when we are fresh. She paused for a moment before amending, "what does everyone else think?"

Jason raised an eyebrow and looked at Garner who was visibly repressing a smile. "I think we'd be safest at their house," he replied.

Jaspreet shook her head, "as much as I want this done, I don't want to be fighting an unknown number of infected possibly at twilight. It makes more sense to find a place to hunker down for the night and then face them in the morning."

"I agree." Garner added, "sorry Jason."

Jason shrugged, as much as he wanted to get there being this close raised the uncomfortable question of what came next. This was his mission but what would he do when it was over? Home was an empty apartment in Toronto. Was he going to walk and steal cars all the way across Canada? Should he follow Jaspreet to Vancouver Island and hope she didn't get sick of him? What did he want?

He wanted to be useful. He wanted to be working on something that would benefit humanity. He didn't want to be wasting time while other people solved the world's mysteries.

"Okay," he agreed, not that anyone had been waiting on his agreement. They had all continued down the tracks toward their destination, heedless of his lack of verbal consent to their plan.

Their path followed along a beautiful stretch of water, gently rippled by the interplay of current and wind. After a while the sun broke through the cloud, sending blinding glints of light off the surface. The road dipped away and returned to the train tracks but both stayed near the river.

The sun worked its path down the sky, shifting lower and lower. Jason wondered if they were on the right path since there seemed to be less rather than more urbanization near the train tracks. Then the tracks curved away from the river and they were in the middle of suburbia.

They stayed quiet and alert for possible infected. The tracks led them between buildings and into an industrial area with wide spaces between abandoned warehouses and moldering machinery. Wind moaned through the buildings and sent leaves and garbage tumbling.

Something fell with a loud bang, sending Jason;s heart pounding. The whole group paused, looking toward the source. A low moan started again and the wind pressed into them.

An infected shambled out from behind a forklift, stumbled over the teeth but recovered with surprising ease. Jaason felt his stomach clench but steadied his hands on his spear. The thing grew nearer and Jason's mind automatically began cataloging its features.

It wore a dirty olive green rain jacket and matching pants with boots so dirty they looked brown with caked mud. It had a welding shield pulled down over its face, though the straps seemed to be cutting into its swollen skin and whatever it had once worn to protect the rest of its head had fallen away. It stretched out toward them with torn work gloves, dragging itself toward them. Its movements showed signs of advanced deterioration, though it seemed determined to overcome that and reach them anyways.

Treegar took a half step toward it but the thing paused and so did she. The low moan it had been emitting peaked into a screech and it reared back, twisting over itself to reverse its movement. It began clawing its way away from them shreiking in abject terror. For a moment they all starred as the thing would back away a few paces and then force itself forward only to retreat again.

Treegar stepped forward and slammed her spear through the back of its skull, cutting off its scream in an instant. Jason stared at the fallen infected as the remnants of its voice echoed in his ears. He squeezed his eyes shut as Treegar wrenched her spear free and shifted back to the group.

"What was that?" Jason whispered. They'd had infected react to them with hesitation and even fear before, but this, this was something more. It had acted, not exactly like it knew Treegar was going to kill it but, as though something about the group elicited an abject primal fear and yet it had tried to force itself through that fear.

"That was dramatic, that's what that was." Jaspreet responded dryly.

"I guess." Jason opened his eyes and looked over at the soldiers, deliberately not looking at the collapsed infected.

"Care to share?" Garner asked.

Jason cleared his throat and looked at Jaspreet before forming his thoughts into words. "Well, you know how previous infected have reacted to us?"

Garner nodded.

"Well, we figured they might have been hesitating due residual signals or emanations from the broken pieces of meteorite we've brought with us."

"Alright, but that," Garner gestured at the fallen infected, "was a little more than hesitation."

Jason nodded, "I know. There is a research group in Europe that found what is essentially an on/off switch in Xeno-1's DNA. It works by manipulating certain levels of radiation. We already knew that radiation affected Xeno-1 but Jaspreet and I theorized that the meteorite pieces must emit some of that radiation naturally, maybe acting as a focus for turning Xeno-1 off." He picked up steam as he spoke, ideas coming together and finding focus through his voice. "If it was meant as a method of clearing the planet for alien colonization then it makes sense that the aliens would provide a method for stopping Xeno-1 prior to their return. This," he repeated Garner's gesture to the infected, "could prove that that theory has merit. We have been reconstructing the meteorite in the hopes that we could trigger this shut off, but it appears that by doing so we have impacted what effect it has on the infected."

"Huh," was all Garner said before turning to Treegar and shrugging. "Alright, let's keep moving. As fascinating as that all is, I'd rather not rely on it as an infected deterrent. If it does have some connection to Xeno-1 then it could just as easily draw more infected to us as scare them away. It's better we get away from here in case this guy was actually calling his buddies for backup."

The group resumed following the train tracks as they reached the edge of a river. "Guess we'll need to either cross here, or" Garner looked over at the large vehicle bridge several hundred yards away, "figure out how to get over there."

Jason looked across the wide expanse of fast moving water, swollen with winter rains and mountain runoff and then to the two bridges. To get to the much wider and safer looking vehicle bridge they would need to backtrack through an unknown city. Would the trade off of time actually lead to greater safety? The narrow train bridge looked less safe but Jason could see straight across it, no infected in sight. The same certainly could not be said about the vehicle bridge.

"I say we go forward." Treegar chimed in when no one else responded to Garner's implied question. Jason nodded and then looked over to Jaspreet. Her eyes were locked on the support boards and the fast flowing water underneath.

"We don't have to if you aren't comfortable." He offered, reaching out and gently touching her arm.

She shuddered but shook her head, " No, this makes the most sense. Let's go." With that she took the lead and stepped out onto the trestle bridge.

It was slow going with the wind buffeting them from every direction. It pulled at their protective gear, wrapped around their legs, slammed into them and then withdrew with no warning. Jason held onto the support posts wherever possible and at a few points crouched low so he could use his hands on the beams and rails for support.

The otherside looked heavenly and Jason and Jaspreet stepped off the tracks as soon as possible to stand on the blissfully solid grass. Garner and Treegar surveyed the area, allowing the doctors a moment to recover and looking for all the world as though their stroll across the open trestle bridge hadn't bothered them one bit.

The group moved on like that, the soldiers remaining on the tracks and the scientists on the usually gravel but occasionally grassy edge, until the tracks split into two. Not much further along it spread into a dozen different lines, all seeming to go in the same general direction parallel to one another.

"Well, do we pick one now or later?" Jason asked the group.

Treegar just shrugged and plodded along in the middle of the spread of tracks.

"Later, I guess," Garner responded.

The tracks led them past dozens of abandoned train cars, moss growing up their wheels and rust forming in their joints. The team crept through the railyard, conscious of the soft crunch of their boots. Past the sitting train cars, the tracks reconverged into one set making the decision for them. The tracks led over an underpass and the group paused to look around them.

"Any idea if we've reached Port Coquitlam yet?" Garner asked Jason.

He shook his head, "no idea. We might need to get off these tracks and look around. For all I know we've gone too far, though

I don't think so."

"Alright," Garner nodded, "time to get off the tracks and take a look around."

Getting off the tracks was easier agreed upon than accomplished. The rail line was protected by a fence, which had probably served to keep people off the tracks and now was keeping their group on them. They could grip through the chain link just fine with their gloves and pass their spears through the holes but their boots had nothing to grip. There was barbed wire at the top of the fence too to add to the overall difficulty.

Treegar went first, lifting her body over the barbs so easily that Jason thought it would be a piece of cake. It was not. All of this walking and food rationing had made him lighter and his legs stronger, but he'd been a teenager the last time he'd had the upper body strength for this. He heaved and pulled himself, his leg scrabbling against the slick metal. The fence shook and clattered, he didn't make it very far up before hands reached out to help him. Jaspreet and Garner pushed as he pulled himself to the top of the fence. Once there he moved slowly, carefully avoiding what barbs he could and trying to remove without ripping what he couldn't. Once his main mass was on the other side, he couldn't stop his body from tipping over and dropping down. Several barbs ripped through the top layer of his clothing. He dangled for a minute from the top of the fence before releasing and letting his body drop. His feet hit the ground and he tumbled onto his butt.

His knee jolted at the sudden landing so he just lay for a moment, waiting for the pain to fade and for his heart rate to settle. Jason rolled over and pushed himself up from his knees just in time to see Jaspreet crest the fence. He looked on in envy and wondered at how both she and Treegar made it look so easy. She lifted her torso over the barbs, catching in a few places but managing to get over and drop onto the otherside with only the sound of one rip.

*   *   *

Vincent was last and while he knew that at one point in his life he could have scaled this fence with the practiced ease that Madison lent the task, it had been many months since he'd done more to work on his upper body strength than their regular carrying and weapons handling. He threaded his fingers through the wire and pulled himself up, the toes of his boots sliping uselessly off of the woven metal. Through agonizing brute strength, he made it to the top of the fence and managed to swing his right foot onto the top bar. The curling barbed wire caught on the cuff of his leg. He was too busy twisting and pulling the rest of himself up to worry about finagling that minor catch out of his pant fabric.

He reached around to the other side of the top bar, bracing his core above the wire as best he could. It caught in a few places but he managed to pull back and release those snags before they caused any real damage to his coat. Releasing his caught right pant leg so he could swing that leg over the barbed wire resulted in a small rip which made Vincent wince. It hadn't hit skin but he knew that any break in his protective clothing was a weakness he did not want to afford. Now that his future held something other than a return to the Canadian Armed Forces he felt a renewed drive to remain safe.

With his body poised half on the train side of the fence and half on the park side, he finally shifted his weight fully over. His left arm swung high, catching the bar near his right hand and finally his left leg began to lift and swing. Vincent couldn't see the moment his pant leg caught but he felt the tug and heard the tear. It was longer than the one on his other leg, large enough that it allowed a flutter of cool air to brush against his shin. In less than a second his body dangling down the fence and he need only release his grip to land gracefully on the ground.

108

He flexed his legs to absorb the impact and spared a moment to assess the damage done to his pant legs. The damage to his left leg was about two inches long with the torn material gaping unnaturally as he moved. He couldn't even see the damage to his right leg and so he dismissed that from his mind for the time being, focusing on how to protect his now much more exposed left leg.

Vincent turned and looked at his companions. Madison gave him a concerned look but he just shook his head, he didn't need her worrying about him right now. They'd been lucky enough so far not to have any real encounters with infected and if that trend held out long enough for him to patch over this pant leg, then there was no point in making a big deal about it now. She turned back to surveying their surroundings and Vincent was grateful for her calm acceptance of his assessment.

They were on a gravelly bump that sloped down into a skatepark with a sparse grouping of tall trees to their left. To the right the park was enclosed by another fence. Across the skatepark was a squat building with a faded spray painted mural.

Their course ahead was so obvious that Vincent didn't bother issuing any orders, it wasn't like the scientists were soldiers anyways and he knew that Madison would have reached the same conclusion as him before he'd even scaled the fence. He simply began making his way to the left and out into the open. Jason muttered something that Vincent couldn't catch but since the doctor had lately begun muttering his more obvious thoughts to himself, Vincent wasn't worried. He was probably muttering about the lack of open, loud, communication. But silence was a valuable commodity that Vincent wasn't interested in losing in case their moment of distraction gave the infected an opening for attack. No matter what the scientists thought about their meteorite, or how it seemed to have affected the infected in the past few encounters, Vincent wasn't going to rely on something he didn't understand for protection.

He led the way through the park, out of the corner that they had entered and over to a large open area with abandoned play equipment. The group spread out slightly, each moving toward something that interested them.

"Lion's park," Madison read aloud, "that mean anything to anyone?"

Vincent shook his head, too busy looking out of the park and past a roundabout. There was a sign hanging above the intersection but at the distance he was having trouble making out was the sign read. Sha... something ending in either a y or a g. He moved closer, sensing more than seeing the rest of the group follow him.

"Shaughnessy!" Jason exclaimed, making Vincent wince at the volume of his voice even though the rational part of his mind knew the doctor was simply excited and speaking at something approaching a normal speaking volume. "That was one of the main crossroads, we've got to be close."

Vincent stretched his hearing to see if Jason's outburst had drawn the attention he most feared, focusing so completely on the immediate danger that it took him several moments to process what the older man had said. They were close. But how close was close? Though the cloud cover made it difficult to see the setting of the sun, the deepening shadows declared the rapidly ending day. "Let's find a place for the night. We can sort out how much further we need to go in the morning." It was the most prudent course and hopefully, the one that would allow him to patch up the hole in his pant leg before they had to deal with the infected they knew were surrounding the sister's home.

The buildings near the park and on the far side of the intersection were commercial or mixed use buildings with their lower windows smashed by looters. The group moved down the road, away from where the train tracks passed, and toward a larger intersection.

"Looks like it'll be less than an hour." Jason announced, his voice once again louder than Vincent wished it would be. He turned and looked at what the scientist was indicating, a sign hung from the traffic lights with a familiar name, "Lougheed".

Jason continued, "They are just down Shaughnessy off of Lougheed. We could keep going."

"We won't have light in an hour." Madison wisely countered.

Vincent was grateful for her intervention though he could see how her tone had bruised the older man's feelings. But since she'd only spoken the truth and allowed him an excuse that wouldn't expose his own vulnerability, he chose not to step in and smooth things over just then.

Jason mumbled something and shrugged, clearly unwilling to speak up and actually counter Madison's argument with one of his own. She, thankfully, didn't dignify his petulance with a response.

"Come on, if they are up that way then we can spend the night in one of those houses and look for them in the morning." Vincent pushed past his companions' conflict with a decision which should provide them with enough security to rest up before tomorrow's confrontation. He had to wonder if Jason was thinking clearly or if his desire to finish his personal quest had made him completely forget that the sisters had said their house was currently surrounded by active infected which their group would need to get through to deliver Agatha's rings.

The more sensible part of him knew that even after everything they had already done, all the distance they had covered, this next section of their quest was probably the most boneheaded. To seek out and voluntarily engage an unknown number of infected was completely idiotic. His personal code forbade him from ditching Jason and his suicide quest but that did not prevent him from thinking about it.

It pained him to think about anyone this way but Jason had been a steady drain on their group. Sure, he was the one with the quest, which had given them direction and purpose. But he was also slow, had few useful skills, and butt heads with Madison, albeit quietly. And Vincent could see the quiet implosion happening inside the man. Literally the only thing keeping him from walking naked into a herd of infected was this request of Agatha's. If that got taken away... Jason would be a danger not only to himself but to everyone around him. He almost wished for a medical problem that Jason could focus himself on, if only to provide the man with some more purpose and use his particular skill set.

Vincent led the group across Lougheed and down Shaughnessy to the first residential intersection. He turned them down the row of houses and townhouses. The pavement was littered with the decomposing bodies. Mostly people but a few lumps that could have once been raccoons or rodents. It was hard to tell which ones stopped due to being shot and which were stopped by some other means but the number of them spoke to someone hunting.

He kept an eye out for any activity from the fallen infected and any hint of movement from the houses. A little over halfway down the street he spotted a row of three nearly identical white houses. The middle one gave him a good feeling. With a silent prayer and the hope that that feeling was the product of inspiration, he turned their group toward it.

He brought them between the buildings along a narrow shared corridor with two paths, each beside their respective house separated by an overgrown gravel patch. He paused at the first window and wiggled its screen out. On the off chance they were very lucky, he tried the window to see if it would open. It didn't. That was hardly surprising but a little disappointing. He lifted the butt of his spear and slammed it into the glass. Again, unsurprisingly it didn't break easily. A white crack marred the glass where his spear had impacted but the glass held firm.

He hit it a second time, a second impact site forming and tiny spidery cracks spreading out. A third hit popped the butt of his spear through the window, his hand sliding forward nearly till his gloves caught on the jagged glass. He pulled his hand back but swept the shaft of the spear around the entry point, widening the hole and breaking off enough of the rough edges that he felt confident reaching through the opening and fumbling around for the lock. The lock flicked up and from there it was simply a matter of withdrawing his arm and sliding it open.

Vincent turned to Madison and found her watching him closely. Even through the visor he could make out enough of her face to understand her thoughts. She wanted to be the one to go inside the building first. He shook his head slightly. She looked pointedly down at his leg and raised an eyebrow. He sighed and nodded. Then tilted his chin toward the front of the house. She shook hers and gestured toward the back. That was in some ways the more risky route as they didn't know what would be back there, but with someone obviously hunting this neighborhood Vincent chose to agree with Madison, entering from the back would be less likely to draw attention if someone was patrolling or watching them.

In moments, without a single word uttered between them, Madison and Vincent had a plan. He stepped out of the way and she grabbed the bottom of the window, rolling her body through the opening and landing miraculously on her feet. She checked the room before waving him off and moving to the closed door.

Vincent gestured for the scientists to follow him and made his way down the side of the house to the gated backyard. Unlocking the gate took less than a second but he was careful to ease it open slowly, listening for the creak of hinges and eyeing the upper windows of the two houses for signs of movement. Someone might still live around here and the last thing Vincent wanted at this point in their journey was to be ambushed again.

The gate creaked momentarily so he let it swing on its own, letting the sound take on the natural tone of something pushed around by the spring wind. When it paused, reaching the point where it might swing back closed, he caught it and held it firm, waving the scientists through into the thankfully empty backyard.

The yard was half grass and half pavement with an electric car still plugged into an exterior outlet. An abundance of garden pots sat abandoned, their fall growth moldering and abandoned. A set of stairs led up to a deck and sheltered two wooden shelving units filled with garden tools and empty pots. Suddenly the door under the deck unlocked and cracked open. Everyone surged to alertness, pointing their spears at the movement and planting their feet. Vincent was happy to include Jason in this moment. Maybe the man would be better off after tomorrow than Vincent gave him credit for.

"It's me." Madison announced, opening the door wider and doing her own survey of the yard before waving them all inside.

The group filed in, Vincent taking up the rear and eyeing the neighboring houses with suspicion.

"Looks like whoever lived here left a while ago, everything looks abandoned. I haven't done more than check some of this floor, so we still need to be alert, but it looks like a good place to spend the night." Madison whispered to the group. Part of Vincent knew that at least in her own mind, this was Treegar and not Madison, but to him the two parts had never really been separate. He saw them as two sides to a coin but all essential to the whole that she was and he couldn't wait for a time when they could explore those halves together.

He shook himself out of those thoughts of the future and stored them away for a later time. They moved as a unit through the house, checking each room and closing doors behind them. The house was empty as Madison had observed, though drawers had been left open and the beds were rumpled and messy. Whoever had lived here had left in a hurry.

"Okay, we should sleep upstairs. The master bedroom looks ideal. Two people can share the bed while one sleeps on the floor and the other is on watch. Any objections?" Vincent looked around at his companions, each of whom shook their heads. "Good. let's get set up, the light's failing and I'd rather not turn on any lights in case whoever's out there is watching."

With that warning the group moved quickly, stripping the guest room beside the master bedroom and moving the extra bedding onto the floor at the foot of the bed. Vincent asked Jaspreet for some of the tape he had seen her with in the van and used a strip of it to cover the tear in his pants on the outside.

By the time they could no longer make out the other side of the room they were ready, boots wiped off and an order arranged for their watches. Jaspreet had volunteered to take the first watch, allowing both him and Madison to snatch some rest after their long day. Vincent fell asleep listening to the muffled sounds of his companions and the near silence created by actual walls.

16

Fear rippled through the virus. It was both acute and inescapable. Something inside of It counted down. It fed with a vengeance, snatching up and tearing through populations with a fervor it hadn't felt since its earliest days. If it grew great enough the fear might lose its power. It segmented itself, feeding with abandon but also searching for the trail of fear, if it could destroy the source, maybe the countdown would stop and it could be free once more.

*　　*　　*

The house felt like it could house two families and still have room to rattle. Madison couldn't imagine living in something like this. She'd get lost in it, feel small. She wanted something that fit her. One maybe two bedrooms, a little kitchen. Something just big enough for two.

Treegar agreed. Small would be more defensible. The extra space in this house made for additional barriers to potential invaders but also spread them out.

Morning broke with a dreary rain. Light sifted through the drops with sluggish reluctance completely at odds with the energy of the group. Treegar had the morning watch and it felt entirely unnecessary. Everyone was awake, fed, and with their bags ready to go before the sun had fully lit the clouds.

The owners had turned the water off before they left, which made sense, if Treegar was going to ditch her house after the US attacked and a zombie apocalypse had begun, she would totally take the time to turn off the water to her house. Not. Who were these weirdos?

A quick trip downstairs for her and Garner resulted in water once again flowing, which was great for both the toilet and the shower. While they waited for the sky to brighten, everyone except her took ten to fifteen minute showers.

The sky was almost light enough by the time it became her turn. She almost said a flat out no but thought better of it. She needed to pee and she needed to try. If she and Garner were going to have a future after this, then it couldn't be one where she only undressed enough for necessities and otherwise remained stuck in these stinking,dirty, suffocating layers of gear.

She went to the bathroom and closed the door behind her. The first thing she did was turn on the shower. The white noise of water hitting tile melded with the sound of rain on the roof. Carefully, with an eye on the closed door, she removed her gloves and held her hand out to feel the water. It was cool but not cold, the sort of temperature you got when a water heater was really trying but you had asked too much of it. She didn't strip down but she did force herself to unlatch her helmet and pull it off. Her hair stuck to it and pulled at her scalp. Unfortunately for her the mirror above the sink was large and unforgiving. She looked like crap.

Her hair was greasy and matted. Her teeth yellowed and in desperate need of a scrub. Her face had ground in dirt that she suspected had been there since her scuffle at Salvation. She pulled her gaze from her reflection and reassessed her surroundings. The small bathroom had a stand up shower, a toilet, a sink, and one small frosted glass window. There was an intake vent in the ceiling but other than that and the closed door there was no way for anything to enter the room.

Treegar sucked her teeth and decided that she needed to do something about her hair. She reached in and turned the shower off and grabbed the shampoo and conditioner and brought them to the sink. There she turned on the hot water and bent over. Washing hair that hadn't been washed in weeks and had been stuck inside a helmet for that whole time was not much harder than she expected. That is to say, it felt like washing a matted, neglected long haired cat. Complete with soap stinging her scalp where chunks had been ripped out and the skin was only partially healed..

The mats refused to come apart even when she soaked them with conditioner. After struggling with that until the water sliding down her neck nearly triggered a panic attack, Treegar wrapped her head in a towel and took a moment to concentrate on her breathing.

Despite the pounding of her heart and the flickering at the edges of her vision telling her brain that she was about to be attacked, she knew that she was as safe as she could be in that little bathroom. She fumbled the water off and sat in the silence, listening for the soft rise and fall of conversation outside of the bathroom door. She had no idea how long she stood frozen, waiting for her panicking, over anxious mind to calm down but eventually the tricks Dr. Rudolph had shown her began to work.

Conditioner drying in her hair and yet still failing to loosen her mats, Treegar rummaged in the cupboard under the sink. Beside the bottles of toilet cleaner and spare toilet paper rolls she found a black fabric bag with what she needed. She opened it and dumped the contents on the counter. Selecting a guard she attached it to the clipper and plugged it into the outlet above the sink. It gloriously buzzed to life. She began combing it through her hair, working around the bases of her worst clumps and leaving only damp stubble in its wake.

With her head bare of all but a shadow of her former hair, Treegar felt liberated, relieved of a stressor she hadn't even been conscious of. Next, she pulled out a left behind toothpaste and toothbrush and set about removing plaque and tartar buildup from her mouth.

She finished by washing her hands and face and then wiped out the inside of her helmet with a face cloth before returning it to her head. Treegar couldn't help but notice the subtle difference in how the helmet fit, the slight looseness around her skull now that she had lost the filler material of her hair.

Last, she replaced her gloves, flexing her fingers in them until they had settled back to feeling like a second skin. With a breath, which smelled of mint inside her helmet, Treegar opened the door back into the bedroom, pausing for a moment as all of her companions turned to stare at her.

For a brief moment fear pricked her skin, had something happened while she was out of the room? Had they been infected?

"What?" She demanded of them, shifting her weight in case they rushed her.

Garner smiled, "Nothing, just thought we'd get to see your new haircut." He cocked his head to the side and wiggled his eyebrows.

"Oh," She answered lamely, forcing her muscles to relax out of their fighting readiness, "I cut it all off. Nothing to see."

"You ready?" Dr. Scordato cut in, practically bouncing on the balls of his feet, his bag already strapped to his back.

Treegar nodded and spared a glance out the window at the increasing daylight. She had certainly taken more than ten minutes in the bathroom. She grabbed her bag and followed the rest of the group as they made their way through the house one last time and back out into the backyard. Dr. Scordato maneuvered his way to the front and Garner slipped back, allowing the older man that position. Madison watched this gentle posturing and smiled at the gracious way that Garner moved aside.

They followed the doctor back up the street and along the main artery. Treegar remained on the lookout for infected but felt her anxiety pricked more by the open black eyes of all the houses they passed. Most looked like they had been abandoned early on while others showed signs that their occupants had remained for some time. Those signs varied from piles of infected at the bases of their walls to nailed up boards and improvised shutters. It was those houses that worried Treegar the most.

She knew they could handle the slow, obvious attack of an infected, especially in the relative open of the street where they would have plenty of warning. But a bullet could take out one of their group before they could blink and she had no way of preventing that.

If the first shot hit Dr. Scordato or even Dr. Nagi, Treegar would be okay with that. But if it hit Garner, that was a different story. She wasn't concerned for herself, death by getting shot sounded a lot better than turning into one of the monsters that had destroyed the world and torn up her mind. But going on without Garner was unthinkable, unbearable.

They were almost there, she reminded herself. One more step and then she and Garner could move forward. And hadn't she just managed over ten minutes with her helmet off? Didn't that prove that she wasn't entirely broken, she could be vulnerable and maybe that meant that their plans for the future were actually viable.

Dr. Scordato finally picked a street and led them down it. There weren't as many dead infected on this street, for which Treegar was grateful. The rain opened up and began a steady beat against her helmet and the ground. The sound muffled her hearing making her swiveling checks of their surroundings imperative to provide any warning of possible attack.

He made another turn and swiftly took a step backward. The group stopped but Treegar felt her already stretched senses go on red alert.

"We're here and they really do have an infected problem." The doctor whispered.

Treegar looked up and met Garner's eye, as one they broke away from the doctors and peered around the bend to make their own assessments. Though it might have previously been a normal house in the middle of this street, the sisters home was now instantly identifiable as one containing living humans. The windows were boarded up from the inside, though Treegar had trouble seeing the outside of the lower windows through the piles of dead and active infected. Even through the rain she could hear a humm emanated from them in a muted echo of their usual moan. She was able to see half a dozen infected crawling over their compatriots to gain closer access to the house.

If Garner would be willing to turn away, she would be halfway down the street with him in an instant. She turned to look at their companions feeling not a flicker of guilt over the prospect of abandoning Dr. Scordatos' quest. But she knew Garner would push them forward, he felt honorbound to this mission and his honor was something she would never wish for him to change. She would never leave him, even if it meant walking toward a literal nightmare.

Lord, she loved that man.

Madison jolted, both halves of her mind having the same thought at the same time. It was strange how planning to run away with him hadn't made her realize the depth of her feelings but this one stupid moment where she knew he was going to do the dumb right thing had made it clear. She couldn't help but smile to herself despite the situation. When this was done, the second they were out of danger, she was going to tell him. It felt too huge and wonderful to keep bottled inside.

Maybe she wouldn't wait until they were out of danger, because that time might never come. Once they were inside that house. That seemed like a more attainable goal. She was going to get them inside that house and then she was going to tell him she loved him.

Treegar pulled her foolish mind from its musings and reassessed the situation. Two soldiers and two semi-competent scientists versus at least half a dozen infected. They might have the advantage of surprise for the initial encounter. And they might have the advantage of whatever the meteorite did to the infected.

She moved back the way they had come, placing distance between herself and their destination. The rest of the group followed her and once she felt they had sufficient space to talk without risking the nearby infected hearing them they began to plan.

*   *   *

Treegar crept along the side of the house, her spear held low and loose but ready to react in a variety of ways if needed. Dr. Scordato moved behind her, matching her pace and posture to the best of his ability. On the opposite side Garner and Dr. Nagi should be doing the same to the house on the other side of the sisters.

As they neared their planned position, one of the windows in the house's second floor opened. Infected surged toward that location. Moments later a long pole poked out, extending to reveal a duct taped joint and a second pole. Treegar nearly laughed as the person wielding the strange elongated spear maneuvered it so that the point fell almost perfectly through the head of an active infected.

Treegar motioned Scordato to pause and they held back while the person inside took out three more infected, one by one. Their instrument was awkward and unwieldy but Treegar respected the effort they were making to defend themselves and the effectiveness of their tactic was clear in the heaps of immobile infected surrounding the house. Now that she knew how they had been immobilized, she could see how they were arranged almost entirely underneath one or another of the house's second floor windows. The few that lay in between seemed to have been rolled there, perhaps due to the movements of their companions.

Something clattered at the other end of the house. Treegar signaled for them to start moving. The infected reacted to the sound the same way they had to the window opening. A handful of them surged in that direction while a remaining three continued to struggle over their fallen colleagues toward the person with the extended spear.

They moved as close as they dared to the house, keeping clear of the mess of decay and ensuring their footsteps made a minimal amount of noise. The infected remained oblivious to their presence though the person inside the house seemed to take note and stopped killing the remaining infected. Treegar jabbed her spear into one from behind. As one the two remaining turned and jolted toward her.

Dr. Scordato lurched forward and managed to plant his spear into a second. The final infected had been closer to the house than its companions and stumbled over a body in its haste toward Treegar. She swept in, briefly stepping in pooling fluids and almost slipping, before slamming her spear into its brain, killing it and stabilizing her own movements.

Their fight was over in moments.

Treegar looked up at the woman, standing off to the side of the open window and saluted her. They then turned and moved toward those that had been drawn off by the noise that Garner and Dr. Nagi had created. Either through the commotion they had caused or the connection that infected seemed to have with each other, they had turned and were making their way toward her and Dr. Scordato.

Garner and Dr. Nagi chose that moment to step out from where they had hidden and toss the reconstructed meteorite into the middle of the fray. The infected reacted as though a bomb had been thrown amongst them, throwing themselves away from it with absolutely no care for their former targets.

It was simply a matter of picking them off after that. In a startlingly short amount of time and with no real resistance they were all immobilized and Treegar's mind was finally able to see beyond their little group.

17

It found the source. Though the virus had felt it for only a moment, it knew. Parts of it that could still move nearby began to converge. It was frustrated at the distance needed to cover, eager to destroy this thing that controlled such a primal fear. The countdown in its mind grew terrifyingly smaller; a frantic sense of urgency scrambled and fractured through every part of it. The virus clawed and scraped for the fraction of hope that destroying the source of its fear might provide.

*   *   *

"Looks like that's it." Garner observed, though his body remained at the ready.

Treegar nodded but could still hear faint moans, whether those were from infected trapped in the piles around the house or from nearby ones that had been drawn by their fight, she wasn't certain but she didn't want a lack of attention on her part to turn this victory into an ambush.

Dr. Nagi picked up the meteorite and held it slightly away from her body as the ichor it had rolled through dripped off of its pearlescent metal. "This worked better than I expected," she observed.

Treegar had to agree, though the why and how were still a mystery to her, and she suspected to the scientists themselves, the strange metal lattice had turned what could have been an outnumbered and potentially suicidal confrontation into something akin to stabbing fish in a barrel.

They turned to look at the next step of their journey. There was a truly stunning number of bodies strewn around the sister's home. Treegar's mind began a quick tally but tapped out after around fifty. Keeping track of them by hands, heads or feet was impossible as their bodies were all jumbled and piled together. Only the few that had rolled away or the nearly dozen that they had just killed were individually identifiable. Bits and pieces littered the lawn and old blood and ichor stained the grass and pavement brown despite the rain's attempts to wash it away.

"Well, the hard part's over, now to get in." Garner jokes.

"Yeah." Dr. Scordato agreed though he made no movement to begin that herculean task.

Treegar moved to the outermost infected body, slammed her spear into it and began dragging it away from the most direct path to the door.

"No point in talking about it," Garner laughed, "let's get to it."

The rest of them joined Treegar in moving the bulk of the infected out of the way so they would have a path to the door. Rain mingled with the bodies, leaving them slick and heavy. Bloat and rot combined to make each corpse a mystery as to whether it would shred apart when you stabbed it or lock together with remaining rigor mortis. With many of the bodies, moving them was only possible as several spears were anchored into them and pulled. It was hard work and Treegar was sweating profusely and regretting her inability to shower.

They pulled one body off another and the arm underneath twitched toward them. Treegar jumped, wrenching her spear from the imobile infected and aiming it at the one underneath. The head was still buried under other bodies but she could hear a faint moaning and guessed at where its head might be. She stabbed, sinking her spear through the main mass of the body atop the moaning one.

The moan shifted into a scream. She yanked her spear free and stabbed again. The scream cut off and the twitching stopped. The group released a collective breath and returned to work.

Blood and rain mingled. Each spear hole seemed to release more rotting liquid into the ground until their boots slipped and the bodies slid nearly of their own accord. Treegar caught Dr. Nagi's arm as her boots lost traction and she nearly tumbled into the body they were moving.

"Thanks." The doctor breathed, quickly righting herself and placing her body at a greater distance from the things she had nearly fallen into.

The work was slow but they were making progress. Only one more body lay between them and the battered front door. Then Garner lost his footing. He went down to one knee, blood, mud, and ichor covering the lower front of his pants. In an instant he jumped back up, reacting as though he had been stung.

*   *   *

Fire raced up Vincent's leg and he had a moment where he knew what was happening.

"No." He croaked, locking eyes with Madison. Good, sweet, complicated Madison. Would she ever know how he felt about her? How vital she was to his life? He suspected, hoped, that he was as vital to hers, but in this moment that brought only despair and fear. What would happen to her without him?

It was over in an instant and he could feel something inside his mind, tearing through his memories with careless abandon. It tore through his thoughts. Madison. Treegar. Kill. Save. Meteorite.

It stopped there to ruminate on what his mind revealed. Vincent struggled to do anything other than submit to the all consuming, overwhelming pain the infection was creating in both his mind and body.

*   *   *

"No." It came out more as a bleat than a cry. Treegar couldn't believe what she was seeing. Garner, something was wrong with him. Through his visor she could see that his face had gone white and blank. She felt frozen. Her fingers limp on her spear and her mouth dry as a desert.

What had happened? Time seemed to move at a snail's pace and yet she knew she was too late. They were almost inside. It was over. No. Her mind rebelled, unable to process what was happening.

He lurched forward and a sound came from his mouth. Not words, but not a moan. Her heart stuttered, had she overreacted?

"G... mmm... nnnn..." The sounds came out, distinct but indecipherable as language, while his facial muscles remained limp.

She should kill him. Stop him. Stop this.

She couldn't muster the strength to lift her spear.

The doctors faded into the background. Her entire world stood, dead and dying, in front of her and she was powerless. Both Treegar and Madison cowered from the enormity of what they beheld.

"Giv... meet... r... nnn... ow." The thing that spoke with Garner's mouth attempted again.

There was a pause and then a third more clear attempt, "Give met...or now." The words, though they were now recognisable as words, sounded nothing like Garner, flat yet guttural, and in that moment of shock meant absolutely nothing to her.

"Give met-or!" the thing that was not Garner demanded, turning and lurching toward Dr. Nagi who stumbled back several steps.

The volume shocked Treegar enough that she stopped staring and looked over at her forgotten companions. They looked just as stunned as she felt.

"G-garner?" Dr. Nagi asked, though her tone implied that she already knew that the being in front of them was no longer their friend.

"Now!" The thing demanded.

"No." Jason whispered in response.

"Give!"

The scientists shook their heads.

"Give us back our friend." Dr. Nagi countered.

The body shook, not just Garner's head but his shoulders and upper torso too, as though it did not know how to isolate and manipulate individual muscle groups. Then it paused and nodded, the motion just as exaggerated as the shake had been. "Give, then I give." It offered.

Treegar looked between Garner's body and Jaspreet. She had no idea if Xeno-1 could leave Garner's body, or even somehow voluntarily give up control. She knew that his mind would be damaged or even dead. Garner would never be Garner again. And yet the slim hope that she might get him back sent tears to her eyes and made her jaw clench until it ached.

Dr. Nagi reached into her bag where she had tucked the lattice before joining in moving bodies. Her body half turned so the contents were hidden from Garner's body but Treegar could see. The doctor reached past the main structure of the meteorite and grabbed something else.

"No!" Treegar gasped, finally tightening her grip on her spear and beginning to lift it.

The doctor looked at her and then nodded, releasing whatever she had been grabbing and instead looping her fingers through the holes in the lattice. She pulled it out, the delicate structure dangling from her hand like spun sugar.

Garner's body flinched and took a half step back. It trembled in a blatant display of fear so entirely unlike the man who used to inhabit that same body.

Something shifted in her mind and she was no longer frozen. She didn't know exactly what she intended but she let go of her spear, allowing it to drop to the disgusting ground and then held her hand out to Dr. Nagi. With her own quizzical look Dr. Nagi placed the structure in Treegar's hand. She looked down at the structure and then back at the clearly terrified being inside the man she loved and felt a cold hatred beyond anything she had felt before. She felt unstuck, free to move because her motivation was clear.

"Why?" The single question dropped from her lips like a rose petal.

"Fear. Give." The thing kept its eyes riveted on the meteorite while it barked its answer.

"Why?" She repeated. She wasn't certain if she meant why did it want the meteorite, or why did it fear it, or even why it had taken Garner from her, all it was was a question because even in her fury she needed to know.

"Death. Fear. Destroy." The thing glanced at the sky, "Hurry! Die! Give!"

It lunged for Treegar, grappling for the meteorite. She pulled away but the thing had already latched onto the lattice. They pulled the thing between them for barely a moment before her fingers slipped, sending each stumbling backwards. Treegar bumped into the door of the house and recovered but the Thing fell onto Garner's backside.

"No!" It screamed, looking at the structure in its hand. "Why? No!" it wailed like a child, attempting to smash the structure on the soft ground and only succeeding in splashing mud and ichor onto the outside of Garner's protective clothing.

Treegar could only watch as this horrible Thing made a marionette of the man she loved. It looked between the structure in its hand and then to the sky, words transforming into unintelligible screams.

The segment of meteorite grew hot in its hand, melting through the glove and scorching Garner's skin. The creature that had been Garner continued to howl, refusing to release the segment of meteorite it held as it burned the flesh of his hand.

Treegar watched in horrified fascination as the piece began to glow white hot, sending the sickening scent of burning flesh into the air, and then pulsed.

The pulse rippled the air, displacing raindrops and passing through Treegar and her companions. Garner's body went limp the moment the pulse released, dropping to the ground as though its strings had been cut.

A second pulse went out, followed by another and another. Treegar took a step away, as did Dr. Nagi and Dr. Scordato. The metal grew too bright to look directly at and the pulses continued faster and faster reaching a crescendo where they were nearly atop one another.

And then it stopped. The last pulse faded and the light and heat emanating from the meteorite did as well. Rain still sizzled as it hit the pieces but within very little time even that stopped. Treegar felt as though a rug had been pulled out from under her.

She felt unmoored. There was nothing in her past experience to provide context for what had just occurred. Her mind flitted through half processed images of what had just happened, unable to reconcile them or make sense.

Anger fled when faced with the enormity of her confusion. Her mind raced on a hamster wheel, doing nothing but replaying the past few moments.

Only one thing could derail her confusion.

Garner.

Her eyes had settled on his body, more out of habit than of hope. With all that filled her mind and the sun spotting of her vision she couldn't be sure of what she saw, until his whole frame seemed to shudder with an indrawn breath.

That sent her stumbling forward, her legs as unsteady as her mind. She dropped beside his body, careful to keep as much space between herself and the meteorite piece that now burned into the ground beside the remaining stump of his hand. Her voice failed her. She grabbed him and shook.

His head lolled. She couldn't feel his heat through their layers of gear. Without a thought she stripped off her glove, and began to work the latch on his visor.

"Hey! No! Stop!" The warnings of the scientists fell on deaf ears. Treegar had to know and did not care about the consequences. The cold and damp of the ground seeped into her legs but her protective pants kept her skin dry, performing their duty for her in a way that Garner's hadn't.

Tears well up in her eyes and her hands shake. It takes her far longer than she wants to get his visor up. When she does she immediately and without thought or hesitation puts her hand on his face.

Someone swore behind her.

His face was cold and damp. A sheen of sweat covered his brow. She reached down, trying desperately to find his pulse. She couldn't reach it and began fumbling to pull his helmet up and expose the zipper and snaps at the top of his coat so she could access his neck.

"She's not?" Jaspreet's truncated question broke the silence.

She ripped his helmet off and pulled down his zipper, running her fingers over his neck in search of his pulse point. She pressed her fingers into his flesh, seeking out any sense that he might have survived. Nothing. Finally she stilled, her fingers resting on his skin, unable to break contact and just watched him.

She breathed, though the air never seemed to reach her lungs. Her heart beat though her blood ran cold. Her eyes remained locked on Garner's pale, still face, unable to properly see it.

Her mind played tricks on her, as it had when it thought that he had moved. For a moment it looked like he released a breath. A moment later he drew another one. Then it happened again. Out and in. Treegar moved her fingers, trying less frantically, to find a pulse.

She had no sense of time, kneeling there, her fingers pressing lightly into his cooling neck, counting breaths that could simply be figments of her imagination. Then she felt something different under her fingers, a new figment. A fluttering beat, slow and weak. A heart beat that moved separate from her own.

She drew in a breath with him and felt it fill her chest. She counted his heart beats and could feel her own blood warming. She smiled and then choked a sob. She reached under his neck and pulled his head on to her lap.

"He's alive." She whispered.

"What?" Her companions questioned, though until that moment Treegar honestly hadn't known if they had left her or not.

"He's alive. He's alive. He's alive." The words poured out of her along with an abundance of tears.

18

The strangers banged on the door. Charissa and Penelope held their guns at the ready and looked at eachother. Charissa had a million questions regarding everything that had happened since these strangers had shown up hours previous but answering them felt less important than defending the children.

"Penelope and Charissa?" A male voice called through the door, "I'm Jason Scordato. I know we got here a little early, but you should be expecting us."

"Prove you are who you say you are." Charissa barked though she did lower her weapon a fraction.

"I have your mother's rings. I'm a virologist. I emailed you regarding your mother's comfort a while back and you told me she likes flowers. I really don't know what else you know about me. I'm sorry, I don't know what more I can say to prove I am who I say I am."

Charissa looked at Penelope who gave her a slight nod. "What was that outside? What did you people do?"

"Look," Dr. Scordato's voice hesitated, "I really don't have any answers. We didn't intentionally do anything. One of us was injured by what happened. He's not infected, I promise." The voice wavered there and Charissa couldn't be sure if it was from concern or if the doctor was hiding something, "But he's unconscious and we need to get him off the ground. Can you let us in?"

That complicated things. If their companion had been on

the ground then he would be covered in potentially infected material. On one hand, Charissa respected the doctor's honesty and wanted to help. On the other, how much was she willing to risk bringing infected material and a possibly infected man into the house? Maybe his gear had protected him, maybe not. And would they even be able to treat his injuries without any of them getting into contact with infected material? It would be a huge risk.

"How can you be sure?" She demanded.

"His skin is the same. Cold and a little clammy, but he hasn't developed the layer of acid that infected have, which means we can check his pulse and touch his skin without being infected ourselves. Until he wakes up, that's the best proof I can give you."

She clicked her tongue and looked to Penelope to confirm her choice. They both nodded. In many ways the decision had been made when they sent the email, today's events only complicated that choice a little. She reached past the barrel of her gun and pulled away the wood that was blocking the door. "We are armed and ready to defend ourselves. You can come in but your boots and any clothing with infected matter need to be taken off in the entryway. That includes your injured friend." She pulled the door slightly ajar and then stepped back up the stairs so she could stand side by side with Penelope but out of immediate reach in case their guests lunged at them.

A moment later the door was pushed all the way open. A person in a military looking helmet and outfit walked backwards through the door carrying the shoulders of a body in a nearly identical outfit minus a helmet. With his head lolling about as his companions carried him, Charissa was able to make out little of their features beyond pallid skin and shaggy brown hair. They reached the bottom of the stairs before Charissa cleared her throat. They and their companions outside the door paused before the one at the front awkwardly forced their feet out of their boots and kicked them to the side.

The pungent odor of feet kept too long contained, filled the entryway, only rivaled by the stench of rot blowing in from outside. A third person, smaller than the first, squeezed their way in beside the person being carried and began removing their coat. It was an awkward process including the usual zippers and snaps but made more difficult as the person holding the shoulders had to move their hands and remove their soiled gloves during the process. Then they removed their pants, which thankfully had a pair of long johns underneath, though they had seen better days as the portions on his shins were ripped and soiled.

Charissa began to feel awkward, standing shoulder to shoulder with her sister, aiming their guns at these people who were trying so hard to do exactly as she had demanded of them while getting their friend to relative safety. Once the man no longer had his pants or shoes, Charissa and Penelope backed up further to allow the soldier space to move up the stairs and into the living room.

"You can take him in there." Penelope gestured to the living room and then followed them to the couch. Charissa hung back and monitored everything from the opening of the hallway. The person who had removed the man's outer clothing closed the door and tentatively propped the chair that had wedged it closed against it. They then removed their own dirty footwear and padded up the stairs and past Charissa.

Only then did Charissa move forward and into the living room after everyone else.

"What happened to him?" Penelope asked.

"He lost his hand in what happened out there." The other man; the one who must by default be Dr. Scordato as Charissa could see now that the person who had carried the man's upper body inside and the one who had undressed him, both women; answered.

"So, he passed out from shock?" Charissa was pretty sure that losing a hand would do that to someone, but what could possibly have caused the burned off stump?

"Maybe." The man unlatched and pulled off his helmet. He was middle aged with sallow olive skin and hair that held more salt than pepper. "Hi, I'm Doctor Scordato, this is Doctor Nagi and our friends over there are Corporals Garner and Treegar. Garner's the one on the couch. We couldn't have made it here without them."

Manners pounded in her by a lifetime of social training kicked in, "Nice to meet you." The sisters chimed, voices overlapping. They glanced at each other and then Penelope took over, "I'm Penelope and this is Charissa." She looked at Dr. Scordato, "You said that you have our mother's rings."

"Ah, yes." The doctor shrugged his bag off his back and set it on the coffee table. He rummaged in one of the side pockets and came out with his fist closed over something. Charissa tensed, raising her gun a fraction. He held out his hand and opened it to reveal two simple and deeply familiar rings.

Charissa sighed and felt grief punch her in the gut. It was true, mom was gone. Nothing could have prepared her for that moment. They'd had so many close calls. So many moments where she thought she knew, thought she had processed her feelings. None of that compared to the confirmation. Mom was gone. She was never going to see her again and there was the evidence right in front of her.

She couldn't breathe. Part of her wished they had left the door closed to these people. Wished she could go back to that tiny glimmer of hope that maybe, just maybe her mom was still out there.

Penelope extended her own hand and the doctor dropped the rings into her palm. Both were careful not to come into direct contact. Charissa was frozen, her gun aimed at the doctor but her hands too numb to pull a trigger.

"Thank you." Penelope spoke for them both. She put her weapon down and looked at the rings. After a moment her shoulders drooped and she held them out for Charissa to take.

Her gun clattered on the floor as she nearly dropped it in her haste to accept her mother's rings. They were exactly as she remembered, right down to the wear pattern from the years of constant wear. She ran her fingers over then, feeling the silky smoothness of well worn metal and feeling her heart break into a million new pieces.

"What happened out there?" Penelope demanded softly.

"We were carrying something we hoped would help in our research for a cure. I don't know why but it suddenly started heating up and then it emitted those pulses. You saw those right?" The doctor waited for Penelope's nod, as though needing that outside confirmation to reassure his own memory. "I don't know what those were. If you'd lend us a first aid kit so we can patch our friend up and then allow me the use of a computer and your internet I might be able to consult with more of the scientific community. I'd like to know what kind of radius those pulses had."

Charissa's attention drifted to where the other doctor and the corporal, the only person in the room with their helmet still on, knelt beside the unconscious man and examined the burnt stump of an arm. The end was a lump of black char with the skin above red and covered with blisters. The effects petered out faster than Charissa would have imagined, only reaching a few inches above the main burn. She would have thought that the heat required to literally burn off a limb would have a larger burn radius, but she really had no idea how close the man had been to the object before it began to heat.

She left then. Feeling a combination of bereavement and anxiety that sent her away from these strangers and down the hall into the bedroom where Sophia and Atticus huddled together. The blankets were pulled up over their noses with only the tops of their heads and their eyes peeking out. They ducked under the blankets for a second and then looked back out, ultimately pushing them down and spearing her with worry in their eyes.

She swallowed the lump in her throat. "It's fine. Your mom's fine. I just wanted to check on you." The words were barely audible but they helped the kids relax. Charissa sat on the edge of the bed, gripping her mothers rings so tightly that they bit into her palm and pulled the children into her.

19

Jason took the night shift watching over Garner. Not that that meant he was alone with him. Treegar refused to leave the room and the sisters seemed equally reluctant to allow their group access to any other parts of the house. So, with Treegar sleeping upright in one of the living room chairs and Jaspreet laid out on the floor behind the couch, not much had changed from previous nights except that Jason was watching over Garner rather than looking out for attackers.

It had taken several hours but the older of Agatha's daughters seemed to tentatively trust him. He'd done his best to explain what happened outside, not including that Garner had been infected, nor the insanity that was the… conversation they'd had with it. With him. Jason wasn't at all sure how to describe what happened. It was so insane that his mind veered away from even the memory of it.

Once the younger daughter had emerged with a first aid kit, he'd be able to clean and wrap Garner's arm as well as check him for other signs of injury. Though Jason hadn't checked his legs until after the sisters had gone to bed.

The infection site wasn't under the large tear in Garner's long johns where Jason had expected to find it. Insead it was on the other leg, just past the ankle. A tiny burn mark surrounded by a halo of pink infection. The burn was no bigger than the end of his pinky. Such a small thing.

He'd done what he could to clean the area and covered it as he had Garner's arm. Though seeing it and remembering what had happened, what he hadn't shared with their hosts, made him wonder if he would be better off killing Garner now than risking him rising again. What if this was simply a state of hibernation? What if Garner was currently asymptomatic but another energy burst would reactivate Xeno-1 and then they'd all be dead?

Jason knew why Garner was unconscious and it wasn't simply shock. He'd seen the CT scans of infected brains. Those were not brains that could be recovered. Xeno-1 had done something different to Garner, it had used rather than destroyed the speech centers of his mind, but that did not mean that there was anything else left. His main hope was that Xeno-1 hadn't had time to cause more than minimal damage. It hadn't been active inside Garner for more than a few minutes, terrifying and frantic minutes but still only minutes.

Jason opened up the laptop that Penelope had lent to him and signed into google. He opened up a blank document and began writing down every single thing he remembered from that morning, in as much detail as he could recall. Here he even included Garner's infection. Lying in his own research notes would do no one any good, not even Garner. He included pictures he had taken of the burned bottom of Jaspreets bag, Garner's arm and even one of his ankle. He had not gone out to take pictures of the meteorite, but made a note to do so in the morning.

Once he had it all written up he opened a second document and rewrote it, omitting Garner's infection. This copy he sent out to all of his academic colleagues, including his government liaison Greg McAlister. Then he went to his favorite forums and posted it there as well.

He checked Garner's vitals, making note of his pulse and respiration and comparing them to the last time he'd taken them. With that completed he returned to the laptop.

Jason missed being part of the academic process. Being part of a community focused on learning and exploration. This crisis, the collapse of the world he knew, and weeks of travel had worn him down so that that life felt years in the past.

He found a thread focusing on the pulses and dove in. There were scientists who had been able to measure various aspects of them based purely on how they'd effected equipment they'd had running at that time. The number of pulses was hotly debated and people had begun listing all the verified effects of the pulses. Just based on the posters and the list of effects, Jason could see that the pulses had circled the globe, apparently becoming weaker in magnitude after they circled back. People were linking this thread back to the mega thread on Xeno-1.

Jason followed that link and read that Xeno-1 had become inactive world wide. People wrote about how lab samples experienced cellular death immediately following the first pulse. Some complained about how it had ruined sensitive experiments. Most just wanted to know how it worked. Some attributed it to the group who had discovered Xeno-1's genetic on/off switch, though replies to those assertions stated that that research group did not claim responsibility and could also not explain the source or nature of the pulses.

It was at that point that Jason decided to circle back to his own post and look at the replies that had been hitting his inbox. They ranged from skepticism to congratulations. Although those that congratulated him also wanted more details into how they had triggered the reaction; something which Jason was fairly certain he had made clear that they hadn't done. He replied and clarified as best he could but it was getting very late and it had been a taxing day so his brain had begun to fog over. When he made three different typos within four words, the only correctly spelt word being 'a', he decided to call it quits.

He clicked away from the scientific forum and over to a news site. Most of the page was pure speculation regarding the pulses and the suddenly inactive virus. But as Jason scrolled a new story loaded to the top of the page.

Invasion Begun

"Around the globe strange pods have landed. At the moment they number in the millions and seem to cover the entirety of Earth's land mass. Grey and approximately the size and shape of an American football, they have yet to do anything of significance other than suddenly exist. However, their arrival within such a short span of time as the mysterious pulses that circled our planet just yesterday leads this reporter to believe the two events are linked. Were the pulses a type of sonar, mapping out ideal locations for these vessels to land?

The article devolved from there into further speculation verging on hysteria but there was included a gallery of these strange objects. They were indeed gray, not silvery, but matte with a shifting pattern. They were oval and based on the other objects Jason agreed with the comparison to an American football. But the objects hadn't landed, exactly. Instead they were each floating about a foot above the ground. The photos came in different qualities and angles, which along with the varied backgrounds emphasized just how many of these things there were. The longer Jason stared at the photos the less he could deny, the shifting pattern on the objects looked eerily like the lattice brain.

*   *   *

Unfamiliar screeches and whistles woke him, sending him lurching out of his chair, almost falling, and definitely tweaking his neck. The noises continued along with occasional thuds and scraping sounds along the side of the house. He didn't know what time he'd fallen asleep so he checked his records for Garner's vitals. The last check was at 3:25am and the time now read 7:13am. Nearly four hours.

Despite the sandy blurriness of his eyes, Jason moved to Garner's side and began taking his pulse. The noises continued during his vitals check though a new lower tone occasionally joined the mix. Garner's condition was unchanged, so Jason took a peek under the bandages. The injury site looked terrible but only slightly more terrible than it had before. Jason removed the dressing and replaced it with fresh dressing. He would have to ask Penelope or Charissa how their medical supplies were if he was going to provide adequate care for Garner.

Treegar stretched in her chair and then glanced around frantically. Jason was grateful when her eyes settled on him already kneeling beside Garner and finishing off his rewrap of his arm. He noticed her shoulders relax lightly before another strange screech sent them back into full tension. He was shocked she could move with how tense she was.

"What was that?" She demanded.

Jason shook his head, "I haven't checked. Garner is stable for now. We need more medical supplies than what the sisters shared with us last night and a way to keep his fluids up." He finished noting the time on Garner's medical notes and pushed himself up, bracing against the arm of the couch to do so. "Let's go see what that is."

Treegar came over and laid a still ungloved hand on Garner's forehead. Jason was still amazed to see her skin. This woman who he had spent weeks traveling with and yesterday was probably the first time he had seen any part of her bare since leaving the Base. He didn't know if it was a good sign or a sign that she had in some ways given up.

He moved over to the covered window and cracked the shutters open, peering through a gap. The world outside was still dark with the earliest glimmer of light peeking on the horizon. Unusual shapes shifted around in the darkness. The longer he looked the clearer they became and what they were doing horrified him.

They were eating the infected.

There seemed to be three different sizes of creatures, though in the low light he was certain that he was missing important details. There was a largish one, about the size of a black bear, that looked like it was leathery with a squat face and large dark eyes on either side of its head and a single line of spines running from the top of its head to a stubby tail. The next creature was about half the size of the largest ones, with long thin appendages. It was covered in either spiky fur or spines, Jason couldn't tell. He couldn't even be certain that the creature even had four limbs because some of them seemed to have five or even six. The smallest creatures were very small, small enough that he wasn't entirely certain of what he saw in the slowly improving light.

Whatever they were they were swarming over and tearing into the bodies of the infected. One of the larger creatures moved away from the feeding frenzy, its bulk seeming heavy and slow for a moment before it paused. The sides undulated and the stubby tail lifted to reveal another creature pushing out. Jason watched as the thing gave birth, a wet smaller version of the mother dropping to the ground. The parent turned and nuzzled the baby, a long tongue slipping out and grooming it. They made their way back to the bodies and the baby latched on to some part of its parent while they resumed gorging themself.

Jason was transfixed. Despite his exhaustion he could not believe what he was seeing. Curiosity and revulsion warred inside but as increasing ambient light revealed more details about these new creatures he found himself incapable of turning away. The hide of the largest creatures varied from pale gray to a light tan. The spines on the medium sized ones, and he was fairly certain that they were spines, were rusty brown but the skin underneath seemed like it might be black. He even caught a few clearer glimpses of the smallest creatures. They looked like someone crossed a fox with a tarantula. It was deeply unsettling.

A wave of fatigue rocked him back and he pulled away from the scene outside. Going back to Garner he rechecked his vitals and then stole Treegars chair. She remained at the window, looking through her own gap in the wooden covers. His mind both rebelled from and could not stop thinking about the things outside. They were definitely not earthly creatures and they were eating the infected. Those thoughts spun in his mind until exhaustion swallowed him once more.

20

*　　　*　　　*

Treegar pushed down her unease as the last sign of the infected were licked off of the front lawn. The last four Littles licked their way through the final ichor and then crawled away on their unsettling eight furry legs. With them gone the front of the house was probably cleaner than before the infected attacked, the only remaining signs of their passage being the defenses the homes inhabitants had erected. It only took those creatures two days of camping outside the house, gorging themselves, and giving birth but now they were done and mostly moved off to find more food. A few stragglers licked and pawed at the siding, presumably to get at whatever droplets of ichor had flowed between the siding and the walls of the house.

She turned around to look at Garner. Dr. Nagi was dripping water down his throat. He still hadn't woken up, if this went on much longer he could die from dehydration and malnutrition. Treegar saw the pity in Dr. Scordato's eyes. There was fear there too.

They needed better resources.

"We need to move him." She announced.

Dr. Nagi looked up from her work and raised a quizzical brow. "What did you have in mind?"

"He needs IV fluids. We need to go to a hospital." She looked down at his pale face and gave in to the strange urge to reach out and touch him, to reassure herself that he was still alive.

"I agree, but how are we supposed to get him there? Do you even know where the nearest hospital is? Do you have a plan for those things outside?"

"We can figure out the logistics before we leave. They do not appear aggressive, and no matter their origin they are flesh and blood so I can fight them. They might be just as scared of us as you are of them." When Dr. Nagi didn't immediately respond Treegar continued, "we have to try."

The doctor nodded, her eyes falling back to Garner's face. "We do, He'd do it for us."

Treegar wished that statement wasn't true. That Garner would place his life before theirs, but that wasn't the case. He'd shown it a million times in a million ways.

"Let's get Jason's thoughts." Dr. Nagi stood up and set the bowl of water and rag aside.

They found Jason in the kitchen having a hushed but pleasant looking conversation with the older of the two sisters. Treegar hadn't seen much of the younger sister since their arrival but that could be given to her own distraction with Garner and the creatures outside.

Whatever the doctor and Penelope had been talking about was cut off the moment that Dr. Nagi and Treegar approached. Knowing that she was emotionally compromised, Treegar hung back slightly and allowed Dr. Nagi to convey what they had just discussed.

"Garner needs intravenous fluids. We need to either move him to a hospital or visit one ourselves for supplies." The doctor was more succinct than Treegar had expected of her, and though the words were phrased as a demand her tone softened them into more of a firm request. Treegar was impressed.

"That makes sense. We shouldn't move him. I don't want to risk aggravating his condition. I'm sure local hospitals have been heavily raided and we can't guarantee the level of infected and the subsequent Bigs, Mids, and Littles. He'll be safer here."

Penelope nodded, "You can leave him with us."

Treegar sent a sharp look at Dr. Nagi, who understood immediately. "Thank you, but one of us should stay with him. It isn't that I don't trust you." she paused and then gestured to Treegar, "It's just that she doesn't."

Treegar punctuated this statement with a slight nod. The sisters were fine, she just didn't know them. What if everything so far had been an act to better even their odds? She wasn't willing to risk Garner on their apparent kindness.

"Oh." Penelope looked at Treegar for a long moment. "I suppose that is reasonable."

Treegar looked at Dr. Scordato, "You should remain here."

His jaw worked for a moment, showing a reluctance to follow her orders that he hadn't displayed with Dr. Nagi's more temperate approach. Eventually he nodded, "that makes sense. I'll do everything I can to keep him stable until you get back."

"So it will just be the two of you?" Penelope interjected.

Treegar nodded while Dr. Nagi shrugged.

"Okay, well…" The woman moved past them and into the living room, "the nearest hospital isn't too far away. At least not by car. I can lend you mine but I have no idea what the roads are like."

Treegar followed and watched her dig around in various places before finding a set of keys. She pressed them into Treegar's gloved hand, "Take these. I'll draw you a map."

She puttered down the hall and into a room that Treegar hadn't seen opened since their arrival. A putrid smell crept out of the room making her wrinkle her nose but Penelope was back in a moment with a blank piece of paper and a pen in hand.

She set the paper on a clear bit of counter space and began drawing. "Okay, this is where we are. You want to go back out to Shaughnessy and then turn up Lougheed." The lines she made on the paper were nowhere near scale and would have been completely unintelligible without her running commentary.

"No." The voice of the younger sister cut in, making Penelope stop her drawing. Treegar turned to look at Charissa. "You're not sending them off with one of your drawings as a map."

"What? What's wrong with my map?"

Charissa stepped closer and made to pick up the paper only for Penelope to snatch it away and hold it away from her sister. "Literally everything is wrong with it. I'll just go with them. I'm a million times better than your *map*, which I can guarantee would have gotten them hopelessly lost."

"It... wouldn't..." Penelope splutters and then looks down at her drawing. "You really suck, you know that, right?" she pursed her lips and glared at her sister.

Charissa nodded her head solemnly, "I do, but not as much as your drawing."

Treegar watched this interplay between siblings with a mild sense of bewilderment. There seemed to be a fair amount of subtext that each sister fully understood but that Treegar herself did not see telegraphed in any way.

"You don't even know where we are going." She observed.

Charissa turned her attention from her sister to Treegar, "I don't but I know the area and I want a closer look at things out there. From what I've seen those creatures don't seem very intelligent. More of a specialized clean up crew for the infected than evolutionarily created creatures. I could be wrong but I'm hoping that understanding them might give me an insight into whatever is coming next."

Treegar nodded, "We are going to the nearest hospital. Garner needs fluids and medical supplies."

"Alright, sounds like a plan. I can get us there." She reached out and snatched the keys from Treegar, "I'll just take these. Give me a minute to gear up and meet me at the front door."

21

Days post Virus- 3

*　　　*　　　*

Volunteering to go out with these strangers was an impulse decision that Charissa wasn't certain she didn't already regret. She hadn't gear up since 'That Day' and while being out of the house was amazing it also spiked her anxiety. She wasn't leaving Penelope and the kids alone this time but she also wasn't sure she trusted the person, people, she had left them with. Of the three conscious strangers they knew Dr Scordato the best.

But she thought she knew Ryosuke. They had met and spoken more than they had with Dr. Scordato, at least before they let him into their home. Ugh, it was a mess. The whole world was a mess.

Although, after all the work the creatures had done, their yard and the surrounding streets were actually much less obviously messy. Dr. Nagi and Corporal Treegar remained silent as Charissa maneuvered the SUV around the various obstacles littering the streets. Despite there being several vehicles abandoned along their route, once they crossed the coquitlam river, Charissa wasn't worried about being able to reach the hospital. There were enough side streets and back routes that she could get them around just about any snarl.

The creatures they'd passed remained consistent with those they had watched at the house and didn't pay them and the SUV any attention. She eased onto the sidewalk to get around a particularly bad section of highway when a Big lumbered out in front of them. It looked at them, turning its foreshortened snout this way and that, the large black eyes on either side of its head glinting in the cloud diffused light. Charissa let the SUV roll toward the thing. The bumper hit and the thing jumped back in confusion.

She hadn't hit it hard enough to damage either it or the bumper but the creature seemed genuinely shocked and scared by the vehicle. It reared up, exposing a pale belly and then pivoted to gallop away. "Well, that was interesting." She mumbled, more to herself than her silent companions.

"Very." The doctor observed. "Did you notice that it had no visible teats? And yet we have observed their young latching to feed. Perhaps teats are a temporary trait expressed only immediately after giving birth, or perhaps they have a different method of feeding their young."

"Or that one was male." Charissa countered.

"Perhaps, I had been working under the assumption, based on observations at the house, that they were hermaphroditic."

"Mmm" Charissa hummed while shifting the car back onto the road now that they were past that particular snarl. Everything about the creatures bothered her. They seemed to be born pregnant, with how impossibly short their gestation periods were and how swiftly they seemed to mature. Each of the creatures she had observed at their house had given birth and then those babies had matured and been eating meat by the time they dispersed. That gave a gestation of a day or less and then a maturation of about the same. It was boggling. That level of population growth simply wasn't sustainable and the consequences of such a boom and bust were terrifying to contemplate.

So she didn't think about them. She pointedly pushed her mind back on to the task of driving and did not think about what would happen if those creatures ran out of food, or when they started to die from hunger.

It worked for a time, easing the car around abandoned vehicles and the collected detritus of a city. She turned off the highway and toward the hospital. The road was clearer here and her mind began to wander again.

She'd never seen one of them poop. Two days wasn't an impossible amount of time to not poop but it was a pretty long time when you were eating as much as those creatures were. She's seen them pee. Was that how they expelled all of their waste? Did the solids turn directly into the creation of a baby?

They rolled past a Mid giving birth while their companions moved out of the way of the SUV. The spindly and elongated limbs looked even more unnatural on the baby than they did on the parent. There were more creatures on this road than there had been on the highway.

The sound of gunfire tore through the air. Charissa slammed on the breaks and looked around. All of the creatures around her did the same, mostly reacting with what she assumed was confusion, not fear. None of them displayed any hint of hostility either toward each other or the SUV. More bangs echoed around them. The creatures shifted but the majority of them returned unphased to their feeding. They had absolutely no fear associated with the sound of a gunshot.

Charissa could not say the same for herself. The last gunshot she'd heard had been from her own hands. Memories of pulling the trigger, of Ryosuke falling, blood pooling around them, their corpses bloated and rotting. Images flashed through her mind, temporarily blinding her to their surroundings.

"North," Treegar observed, the soft alto of her voice pulling Charissa out of her flashbacks.

"What?" The question was out of her mouth before her mind had the chance to process what Treegar had said but by the time her mind had done its processing Treegar was already clarifying her statement.

"The gunshots are coming from the north. We should proceed with caution."

Charissa nodded and eased her foot off the brake to let the SUV roll forward. The creatures ahead of them shifted out of the way. As freaky as they were, Charissa did not want to find out if the Mids spines would puncture tires or what it might feel like to run over a Little.

She turned into the emergency entrance, pulling on to the winter flattened lawns to pass backed up ambulances and other vehicles. Driving along the sidewalk got them as close to the Emergency entrance as she possibly could. The glass panels of the automatic doors had been smashed, with the fallen bits showing the cloudy pock marks of the infected acid. Charissa could see several creatures, mostly Littles, inside picking through the debris and licking heaven only knew what off of anything that interested them. None of them knew how the creatures would react to living humans, especially when their diet seemed to consist primarily of dead humans.

More gunshots echoed off in the distance, though it seemed they were growing further away. By silent mutual consent each woman cracked open their door at the same time and began to ease them open. Charissa stepped out of the SUV, glass crunching under her boot. Several of the Littles turned to look at her their eyes a glimmering amber in the shadows. She froze, poised to leap back into the vehicle should the creatures attack. In a heartbeat most of them returned to their scrounging but one skittered closer. As slowly and smoothly as she could Charissa shouldered her gun and took aim, ready to shoot the disgusting thing before it might harm her.

The creature's ears swiveled back and forth, its big eyes seeming to grow more brown as they focused on her. The snout which looked more pointed than its companions twitched. It paused for a moment, two of its hind legs flexing, and then in a blink it turned and rejoined the others.

Charissa released a short breath and finished easing her body out the door. In an attempt to minimize noise she and her companions slowly and softly closed their doors.

Gathering together in a loose triangle, they proceeded past the Littles and into the hospital. The Littles ignored them completely with the exception of shifting away should they ever get too close to one of them. Charissa noted this display of indifference and filed it away for further consideration. They made their way deeper into the building, automatic lights occasionally flickering to life as they passed their sensors.

Another group of Littles was working away at the remains of an infected. They reacted for a moment but similar to the first group, only one paused to sniff them and then the whole group dismissed them. Charissa was beginning to suspect that something about their smell signaled that they were neither a threat nor of interest to the creatures. She wondered if that would hold true for the Mids and the Bigs.

They found a supply closet that had been opened and ransacked. Still, they stopped and investigated. General supplies seemed to have been completely removed, however IV lines and poles had been left virtually untouched. The soldier and doctor grabbed these while Charissa kept an eye out for any hostilities.

The Littles were making their way deeper into the building, following behind their group but in a way that didn't appear related. Charissa still kept an eye on them, just in case.

"Let's keep going." Treegar whispered, carrying the few supplies that she and Dr. Nagi had chosen.

Charissa nodded and followed along, allowing those who cared and knew what they were looking for to lead the way.

They passed an almost untouched infected and the Littles who had been moving along behind them converged on the thing, tearing into its rotten flesh and releasing more of its putrid smell. Charissa gagged and turned away.

They moved away from the horror scene toward what the signs declared as the emergency OR. There they found another storage room, but this one had several infected bodies tangled up in its doorway. One of the bodies looked particularly fresh, as though the person had been infected only hours before the Pulse.

Treegar used her spear to almost vault over the pile, landing just past the jumble inside the closet. Despite the door being open, the closet appeared nearly untouched. Even from the hall Charissa could see organized boxes of medical supplies filling nearly every shelf. Treegar looked through the offerings before grabbing a heavy looking one and holding it out the door at Charissa.

"Take this." She ordered.

Charissa reflexively accepted, allowing her rifle to swing on its shoulder strap so it rested along her back. Treegar shoved another box at Dr. Nagi then grabbed a third, vaulted back over the pile with the box in one arm, and set off back to the vehicle. Charissa had to admit, it was pretty cool. Dumb, cause Treegar could have slipped or dropped everything, but cool.

The Littles had already made some serious headway into disposing of their infected body. And in the short minutes since they'd left them, the Littles had already multiplied with two of the largest adults now having babies attached to their underbellies. Charissa craned her neck to get a better look at the connections, trying to make out if there was a nipple for the babies to feed on but couldn't get a good enough look.

They dropped the boxes in the back of the SUV and returned inside. As they passed the Littles, one of the babies released its hold on its parent, revealing something between a nipple and a bite. Liquid oozed both out of the protrusion that might be a nipple and from a crescent of punctures above.

This time Treegar used her spear to leaver the freshest body out of the doorway. Their mass caught on the infected below and Treegar was forced to drag both if she wanted to move one. With no tool to help both Dr. Nagi and Charissa watched Treegar move them out of her way in almost no time. Then she only had to step over their remaining goo to enter and exit the closet.

They emptied the storage room of everything, obviously useful or not, and packed it into the SUV. With the room empty and the vehicle filled almost to capacity, Treegar finally seemed satisfied.

"Let's head back." She ordered.

Charissa was starting to dislike this woman's manner of leadership but since she was anxious to get home and her arms were tired she didn't argue. In the time it took them to unload the storage room the Littles had had two more babies and the first babies had stopped drinking from their parents and begun eating the infected. They had also grown at an alarming rate, having more than doubled their birth size. She hadn't known that what she'd seen was possible beforehand.

As they loaded the last boxes into the back of the SUV another series of gunshots tore through the air. The volume declaring their proximity to be much closer than the previous shots. Charissa rushed to the driver's seat and turned the vehicle on, throwing it into reverse even before her companions had fully closed their doors. The very last thing she wanted to deal with right now was whatever lunatics with guns were out there right now.

She backed them out from the Emergency entrance and

managed to turn around on the lawn. She followed the same path she'd used to get them there rather than risking some of the openings that looked better but might be blocked further along.

Just before the bridge she thought she saw another vehicle moving and hit the brakes. Neither of her companions questioned her actions, instead joining her in peering out the windows for any hint of human activity. It was then that Charissa saw someone in the distance, creeping through the bushes beside a row of townhouses, a rifle held low at their side. She swallowed and leaned back in her seat, keeping her one eye on the person and scanning the area for any companions. Even with the threat of the infected gone, she couldn't imagine any but the most desperate venturing out alone.

The person slipped away through the bushes. Their absence made Charissa's heart pound more than seeing them had. She waited, long after they were gone before easing her foot off the brakes and allowing the SUV to roll forward as slowly as possible.

They inched past another car, rolling in front of the bushes that the person had disappeared into. Charissa held her breath, wishing that she could both drive and have her gun ready to shoot. Long tense moments passed.

Bang!

The sound of a shot firing coincided with a bullet hitting the side of the SUV.

Charissa slammed her foot on the gas and the vehicle lurched forward. She had to swerve around several other cars, moving in quick succession at the increased speed of the vehicle but adrenaline helped narrow her focus on getting out of there and away from their assailant.

They were over the bridge and turning up Shaunessy before she had a moment to think. Someone had shot at them. Someone had seen them.

Anxiety steadily built in her chest. Her eyes strained around corners, even though she knew that the house was far out of view and their assailant must be far behind. She kept checking and rechecking her mirrors and windows, noting how Treegar and Jaspreet were doing the same. The final turns toward the house seemed to take forever despite Charissa keeping the SUV moving at a faster pace than she had for the majority of the trip.

Turning to see the house was the worst thing she could have imagined as more creatures had taken up residence on their lawn and were happily devouring bodies that hadn't been there when they left.

22

Day's post Virus- 3

*   *   *

Jason watched the SUV pull away and then turned back to do another check on Garner. He already suspected that all this effort was pointless and the past two days had simply confirmed that for him. For now he could only keep Garner stable and hope that Treegar would reach the same conclusion before Garner actually died.

She had been weird before, but now she was fully fixated on Garner. Jason worried about what she would do if she thought that Garner was really gone. So, instead of offering his medical opinion, Jason checked his vitals and prepared to change his bandages.

Only prepared though because a look at his supplies showed him that he'd need to ask his host for more. Penelope wasn't in the kitchen and didn't respond when he called out for her so he went looking. He made his way down the hall, stopped at the first door and knocked. There was no answer so he gently turned the knob and eased the door open. A stench so pungent and horrible it immediately made his stomach lurch hit his nose. He closed the door and bolted to the kitchen sink, dry heaving and spitting to remove the taste of the smell from his mouth.

"What in the world..." He muttered to himself. What was in that room? He rinsed out his mouth and blew his nose as much as possible then resumed his search for Penelope.

162

"Penelope?" He called loudly, and then again louder. "Penelope!"

"What?" She demanded, pulling the third door down the hall closed behind her.

"What is in this room?" He gestured to the first door.

Even in the dim light of the hall he could see her face grow slightly pale. "What do you mean? What are you doing looking around my house? Haven't we been doing enough for you? What more do you want?" Her questions turned into accusations and Jason could feel himself getting pulled off track and into a more defensive position.

"I was looking for you. What stinks so much in there?"

She went quiet then her shoulders slumped. She gave the room behind her a quick glance and then motioned for him to move back down the hall to the living room. "I'll tell you but you need to hear me out."

They sat and Jason crossed his arms, waiting her out as she clearly struggled to form her explanation. Penelope picked at her fingernails and stumbled through her words, "You need to understand that we were attacked." She took a long shuddering breath, "Timothy and Charissa were out clearing the yard when they hit. We... I... I hid in the bedroom and didn't challenge them but when Tim and Charry got back they fought. S... I was threatened and Tim was trying to deescalate the situation when, well, I don't know if the guy shot first or if Charissa shot him and then he fired. Either way, he died and so did Tim."

She looked deflated as though saying all of that had taken the wind out of her.

"So, it's your husband in that room?"

She shook her head, "No, he's in..." She paused and seemed to be searching for the right word, "he's in the fourth room."

"So, that's the guy that attacked you?"

She nodded and then ended with a small shake, "That's two of the people who attacked us."

"You and Charissa fought off two attackers?" Jason was impressed, he hadn't thought these women would have had that in them.

She looked away, "Sort of. Charissa took care of those two. There are three more in the basement."

"What!" Jason stared at her in shock. He'd spent three days in a house with, he quickly counted to make sure he was correct, six, SIX corpses.

"We couldn't get rid of them. The infected swarmed us almost as soon as the guns went off. There was no where to put them, and honestly, without Tim… I just didn't know what to do."

"Did I count that correctly? You fought off five attackers? And your husband, I am so sorry." Jason wasn't sure how to handle this situation. In all his years, no one had ever confessed to murder, or did self defense make it manslaughter, to him before and he was struggling to find the right reaction.

"I think I only killed two. Charry, she was amazing. Without her, we would have lost everything. The…" She hesitated, "the food, all of our supplies. They would have left us to starve and be infected." She swallowed and glanced down the hall. "We need to get them out of the house. I know we do. And we can now. I don't care if those creatures eat the attackers but I…" she struggled with her words for a moment and Jason just waited as she worked out what she wanted to say. "I want to give him a proper burial. I couldn't stand to see him eaten by those things."

Jason nodded, that sounded reasonable.

"I know it is a lot to ask, and it isn't why you stayed here I know, but would you help me move them outside?"

Just the memory of how they smelled sent Jason's stomach rioting but she looked so small that he couldn't stop himself from nodding. At least if he helped her remove them there would only be one corpse left in the house. His gaze drifted to Garner. Maybe two.

*   *   *

He put his gear back on and tied a cloth over his nose. The mud and gunk on his boots had mostly dried and fallen off over the past few days but he was still careful to put on his gloves and watch where he touched before pulling them on. Penelope joined him wearing her own hodgepodge of protective gear and carrying a folded sheet.

"I thought we could put them on this, it might make it a little cleaner."

Jason nodded, the sheet should catch some of the fluids and then they wouldn't have to risk the bodies falling apart as they carried them.

They went to the door and Penelope opened it. Jason kept his breathing shallow to protect himself from the stench but there was nothing to protect him from the sight. The bodies were still clothed in their own protective clothing though their skin was discolored and bulged from every possible spot. Fluids had pooled underneath them in a thick sticky mass. The room around them was a shocking contrast with childrens toys and brightly painted walls.

"Okay…" He muttered and reached out to Penelope. She handed him one side of the sheet and he pulled it along behind him as he stepped around the pool to the heads of the bodies. They further unfolded the sheet and laid it down beside the left body. The center of the sheet quickly stuck to the fluids and absorbed some of them creating a discolored patch. Together Jason and Penelope rolled the body onto the sheet. The flesh felt weirdly soft and strange through their clothing but Jason tried to push that out of his mind and focus solely on the task at hand.

With the first body on the sheet, Jason wrapped the corners of the sheet around his gloves and then he and Penelope lifted the body off the floor. It slid into the center of the sheet, creating a deep U shape. With effort they were able to keep the body from dragging along the floor. Jason stepped through the puddle of fluids, his boots sucking and squelching with each step.

They set the sheet down and rolled the body off before picking the sheet back up and repeating the process. With both bodies out of the children's room, because Jason was certain that that was the previous funcion of that room before it became a mortuary, they moved down to the basement and began moving those bodies as well. It was significantly harder getting the bodies up the stairs to the front door than it had been bringing them down to it.

Jason tried not to look at the faces under their various face shields. Those who had been laying on their faces made that easier by their fluids discoloring the plastic. Bloat and decomposition helped him to see these as just bodies and not as people. Medical school and practicing on cadavers felt a million years ago but he pulled on the dispassion he had learned at that time to muscle through this task.

The last body was smaller than the others, which was a blessing as Jason's arms were very tired, but also a worry. He could no longer tell if this person had been a teenager or a woman or just a small man, but somehow it left him further unsettled.

Creatures were regathering on the lawn by the time they made it outside, which made the pair hesitate. Several Littles were picking away at the furthest away body. Unwilling to get into a fight with them, Jason and Penelope dropped the final corpse just out of the way and left it wrapped in the sheet.

On their way inside, Jason bent down and pulled the meteorite lattice from the hole it had burned in the ground, leaving the smaller fragments for future collection. The pearlescent sheen of the metal was obscured by carbon, the remnants of either Garner's hand or the soil it had fallen into and subsequently incinerated.

Once inside the house, Jason opened up his coat and let the cool air hit his core. He wasn't sure if the house reeked of death due to them moving the bodies or if their stench just clung to him but Jason hated it. There was a trail going up and down the stairs of boot prints and old blood overlapping each other along with droplets where the bodily fluids had dripped from the sheet. It was a disgusting mess.

"I'll get a mop." Penelope sighed. She made her way up the stairs, needlessly avoiding the trail and instead leaving little half prints from her own boots.

Jason took a deep breath and gagged, barely catching the bile half way up and forcing it back down. It was disgusting, his throat burned and tears sprung to his eyes. But he got control over himself again and focused on keeping his breathing shallow.

Penelope returned with a bucket and two mops. She set one mop down at the top of the stairs and then followed her own footprints back to the entryway with the second mop and the bucket. "I'll start upstairs if you're okay starting here and working your way down. I'll join you when I'm done up there. Just get the worst of it. We can go over it again after. I am so sorry. Thank you for helping with this." She sounded exhausted so Jason just accepted the bucket and mop and kept his reply to a nod.

The clean up wasn't as gross as moving the bodies. He started with the landing which was far worse than the stairs because not only did it have the fluids and boot prints from today, it had the dried up residue from three days ago and whatever had been there before that. Garner's gear had been hung and his boots neatly placed aside but the mud and gunk they had brought in with them meant that Jason had to change out his water before he had finished cleaning the landing.

The stairs were a piece of cake by comparison.

And then he made it to the basement floor. He had to change out the water again by that point and went up stairs to dump the bucket. Penelope had cleaned up the upper stairs and the hallway to the room. Jason glanced down the hall, not really expecting to be able to see anything since she should be in the first room cleaning the floor. Instead he caught the third door being closed.

He paused for a moment, it was strange for her to be going into her bedroom in the middle of cleaning up these bodies. Then he heard a noise from the first room. Curiosity got the better of him and he tiptoed to the open door. There she was cleaning the floor. She looked up and gave him a weary smile. "How's it going down there?" If her eyes hadn't darted behind him, he might have written off the other door closing as a trick of his mind, but it was finally clear that there was more that she was hiding.

"It's fine, just getting fresh water." He tried to keep his tone light though now that he thought about it it was obvious that the sisters had been hiding things from them all along. He'd just helped her dispose of five bodies for heaven's sake, what part of that made him think that these women deserved the trust he'd been giving them. They might be Agatha's daughters but they definitely had secrets, at least one of which was that there was at least one other, living, person in this house.

"Good luck down there." She smiled at him and then returned to her cleaning efforts. Jason pulled away and went to the bathroom, dumping the bucket in the tub and waiting for the water to drain before setting the bucket down and running the water to refill it. He considered sneaking down the hall and finding out this new secret but thought better of it. If Penelope was hiding someone he would much rather confront her about it once Treegar and Jaspreet were back, something to even the odds and as much as he wasn't sure about Treegar's mental state he knew he could trust her to back him up as long as he was taking care of Garner.

23

Days post Virus- 3

* * *

This past week has been something else. Greg looked out his window at the scavenging creatures that appeared approximately twelve hours after the Orbs, which had in turn appeared about ten hours after the world experienced a series of pulses and Xeno-1 suddenly stopped. If he hadn't received an email directly from Dr. Scordato regarding the pulses before the Orbs or the creatures arrival, he wouldn't have believed him. As it stood they now had a totally different problem than the one they'd been facing before.

These creatures were roving the planet devouring the dead. The funny thing, as far as he was concerned, was that they were in areas unaffected by Xeno-1 as well as those devastated by it. They didn't care at all about anything living but went out of their way to find and eat anything dead. To the point where they had already dug up and consumed thousands of cemeteries and graveyards.

They reproduced without any form of sexual activity, in fact they seemed to care about as much for each other as they did for living humans and animals. The main problem with them was two fold. What would happen when they ran out of food? And what did their presence mean about the future?

If Greg thought he could survive outside in this new world he would just walk away from his job. He was so done. Done with wearing the same gross clothes over and over again. Done with sponge baths in the office bathroom. Done with sleeping on his couch. Done with being the guy who was somehow still in charge of managing this ongoing disaster.

But he knew he wouldn't survive out there. The creatures might be harmless but the people had begun to turn. No longer afraid to go outside they were now roaming in packs, looting and taking whatever they wanted.

He'd heard of some of them trying to eat the new creatures. That was a bad idea, as scientists had found out within 24 hours of the first creatures appearing. Every aspect of these creatures was foreign to the human digestive system. They weren't exactly poisonous to us but our bodies treated them in much the same way as if they were. So, despite their abundance, the alien creatures would not feed the starving masses and they were beginning to fall on each other.

*   *   *

Treegar's only concern when the car screeched to a stop in front of the house was checking if any of the bodies being eaten by the creatures was Garner. The moments between the car halting and when she stood beside the last of the bodies were a blur of relief. Garner wasn't among them, not unless he had changed gear and undergone far more decomposition than was possible in the hours they had been gone.

With that established she returned to the car where Dr. Nagi still stood, in shock. Charissa was standing in the open doorway talking with her sister, gesturing wildly and clearly agitated. Treegar couldn't care less what the sisters were arguing about but definitely wanted them to get out of her way so she could carry the medical supplies up to the living room and actually reassure herself that Garner was in fact, okay.

She grabbed two boxes and walked to the door. "Move." She ordered, pausing only a moment before stepping forward to force the women to give her space.

"Hey, just wait a second!" Charissa snapped.

"Move. You can talk somewhere else." Treegar stepped forward, forcing the other women further into the house. They chose to shift down toward the basement, which was smart since Treegar had no interest in going down there.

The first thing she did once she set those boxes down was check that Garner was still breathing. The steady rise and fall of his chest doing a lot to ease the tension within her. Dr. Scordato was nowhere to be seen and at first that didn't bother her, but by the third trip she had begun to worry. She took a moment to check Garner's pulse and temperature, both of which seemed fine.

"What do you think happened while we were out?" Dr. Nagi whispered after setting down her latest box. "Where did those bodies come from?"

"Probably the first room down the hall." Treegar answered calmly. The smell she'd caught when Penelope went in there earlier to get a pen and paper made more sense now. She didn't know how they'd gotten to the lawn but that hardly mattered. What mattered now was unloading the vehicle and finding Dr. Scordato so he could set up IV fluids for Garner. She didn't know the first thing about putting needles into people and she was pretty sure Dr. Nagi didn't either.

"What!" Dr. Nagi sputtered, starting and stopping several words with only the first syllables formed, "h…. wh…. tha.." she finally stopped and took a breath, "How long have you known there were BODIES in that room?" She gestured toward the hall.

Treegar shrugged, "A few minutes ago." She kept talking while walking back to the car, Dr. Nagi trailing behind her. "Penelope opened the door before we left and I could smell decomposition. I didn't think anything of it since, well, everything usually smells like rot. I didn't make the connection until I saw these guys out here."

Dr. Nagi seemed to be taking several deliberately deep breaths while glancing between Treegar and the bodies which were rapidly being overrun by the creatures. "And it doesn't bother you that they were hiding five bodies in the room next to where we were sleeping?"

Treegar shrugged, she hadn't gotten that far in her processing. She was focused on getting Garner better, not on the morality of their hosts or their questionable storage choices.

Dr. Nagi threw her hands up, "You know what, I don't get you. This is insane and you're acting like it's nothing."

Treegar picked up the next box and let the doctor have her hissyfit.

"How does this not bother you? Are you even human?"

That made Treegar pause. Maybe all Dr. Nagi needed from her was a reaction because she fell instantly silent, allowing space for Treegar to respond. "I can't let it bother me right now. Garner needs me, he needs this place. We have all done terrible, insane things and it would be hypocritical of me to start pointing fingers and freaking out right now. I will deal with the ramifications of this development once Garner has what he needs." She stated her piece calmly then resumed bringing the box inside.

She set that box with the others then turned to get another. Dr. Nagi was coming up the stairs with a box, so Treegar waited to pass.

"I'm sorry, I got carried away."

Treegar nodded. She knew she was odd. That she was broken. She knew that separating herself as she had was neither normal nor healthy. But it was the only way she had been able to get through everything. The past months would have been easier if she wasn't human, if her mind and heart didn't feel and hurt so much.

She grabbed two more boxes from the trunk, leaving only one more and an IV pole inside. The Bigs who had joined the Littles and Mids looked up at her for a moment then returned to their eating. She passed Dr. Nagi in the entryway and heard the SUV trunk close after she set her boxes down.

She pursed her lips at the continued absence of Dr. Scordato and set out to find him. She went past the kitchen and into the hallway. The door to the first room was open with a bucket of brown water and a mop sitting beside a partially cleaned pool of goo. It was smaller than she would have expected for five bodies but Treegar didn't dwell on that fact and continued down the hall.

The bathroom was empty, but to be safe she walked in and checked in the tub and behind the shower curtain. Which she knew to be ridiculous because why would Dr. Scordato hide behind a shower curtain?

Next she went to the third door. The moment she cracked the door open a soft susurrus of voices inside stopped. Treegar pushed the door wide and looked inside. The room was primarily lit by a large TV screen which spilled light directly onto a heavily blanketed bed. At the head of the bed two little heads peeked out at her.

Madison stepped back. Children. They'd been keeping children in the bedroom. She'd been in this house for three days and hadn't seen them, which meant they'd been trapped in here for that whole time, maybe longer. She was outraged and hurt and desperately wanted to make sure they were okay. The sudden emotions swamped over her and Treegar squished them down.

"Who are you?" Her voice came out harsher than she had planned.

The children looked at each other before the girl lifted her head and replied, "Where's our mommy?" Her voice was small with a hint of fear which broke Madison's heart.

"Oh." Realization swept away her earlier emotions. That was the voice of someone who fully expected Treegar to be the monster that had already killed her mother. It felt like a gut punch and she knew she needed to do anything she could not to be that monster. She reached up and unlatched her helmet, pulling it off and placing it under her arm before answering. "Your mom is fine. She's downstairs. I'll go get her for you." She closed the door and fled down the hall.

Treegar replaced her helmet, not entirely sure what possessed her to remove it even for that short moment. She moved quickly down to the basement where everyone else was in the middle of a rapidly escalating argument.

"How can we trust you?" Dr. Nagi insisted, "You claim these people attacked you but you've got no evidence to back that up! You've been hiding their bodies since before we got here. Are you even Agatha's daughters or are the real Penelope and Charissa out there!" She pointed to the front of the house.

"What!" Penelope gasped, apparently horrified at the accusations Dr. Nagi was throwing around.

"You know what!" Charissa cut in, her voice and tone rising with each word, "You can just leave. We don't have to prove ourselves to you or anybody and we certainly don't need your judgment!"

"Excuse me." Treegar cut in only to be spoken over by Dr. Scordato.

"What else are you hiding? I know there's someone else in this house! You've been cutting out parts of your story and I know I saw someone upstairs!”

“Excuse me!” Treegar yelled, pitching her voice to carry. All parties looked at her with annoyance. She faced the sisters, unsure of which was the children’s mother. “I startled your children and they need reassurance that I haven’t harmed you.” She stated this calmly but by their reactions you’d think she had tossed a flash grenade at them.

“Oh my!” Penelope gasped, rushing past Treegar and up the stairs almost before she’d finished her sentence with Charissa only a half step behind.

“Children?” Dr. Nagi and Scordato echoed each other.

Treegar turned to the now dazed doctors. “Garner needs your attention. I trust that whatever this was can wait until he is receiving proper fluids?”

“Right, yes. I’ll be right there.” He looked every bit as dazed as if he’d been struck on the head.

Treegar decided that he might need a moment to recover and returned upstairs, moving down the hall to overhear what was being said in the bedroom.

“Who was that?” One of the children asked

“A soldier, they’re here to protect us.” Penelope explained.

“Why are they here now? Why didn’t they come sooner?” The other child countered.

Treegar shrunk back so they wouldn’t know that she was there.

“They couldn’t. They were a long way away and had to walk a lot of the way here.”

“What about the monsters? And the bad people? Weren’t they scared?”

"I'm sure they were. But they knew you needed to be safe so they came anyway."

"Why couldn't they be here to protect daddy?"

Madison felt tears begin to fall from her eyes, catching at the bottom of her helmet.

"I don't know everything that happened on the way here. I just know that they tried really hard to get here as fast as they could."

"Will they keep us safe?"

"They'll try. But even if they can't or if they have to leave, you still have mommy and auntie. We aren't going to let anything hurt you. Come on, are you ready to meet them again? And they have some friends, a doctor and an astronomer. And they have a friend who got sick on his way here, he's sleeping on the couch right now so we need to be quiet, okay?"

Treegar slid down the hall into the living room just as the doctors came to the top of the stairs. She turned away from them so they couldn't see her face through her visor and moved to Garner's side.

Scordato and Nagi looked behind them and paused, obviously staring at the two kids who were equally staring at them. Somehow it was less rude coming from the children.

Treegar cleared her throat, "Doctor, if you don't mind, I think Garner has waited long enough." She pitched her voice to be light but firm, hoping she wasn't retraumatizing the children.

"Oh, right." Dr. Scordato jumped and went over to the pile of boxes and dug into them. Treegar openly watched him work while Penelope and Charissa worked the children down the hall. Scordato opened and looked through several of the boxes, pulling out various tubes and packages before he brought his findings over to Garner. He hesitated for a moment and looked at

Treegar. She couldn't quite read his face as he searched hers for a moment before continuing to his task.

That look brought up some of her anxiety and she watched him even more closely as he set up the pole, hung a bag on it, plugged the tube into it and worked the air out of the line. Then he bent to Garner, lifted his uninjured hand and placed it on his chest. He then pulled a packed needle from his pile, opened it, and pushed it into a vein in the back of Garner's hand.

Treegar had been so focused on Scordatos' movements that she hadn't been monitoring the children's progress. By the time he straightened up and checked that everything was working correctly, she noticed that they had reached the top of the stairs and were craning their heads around the couch to see what Dr. Scordato was doing.

"You wanna ask what he's doing?" Charissa stage whispered to the little girl.

The girl nodded her head and then shook it.

Penelope knelt down and looked her children in the eyes, "You don't have to talk to them if you don't want to but we should at least wave hello."

The little boy took that very seriously, quickly turning and waving at them all and then darting behind Penelope before anyone could wave back.

Madison smiled and waved anyway.

"Why are you wearing that?" The little girl blurted out. "You took it off before."

Treegar froze for a moment before pushing herself through her discomfort. She knew she needed to get used to taking the helmet off. Garner wanted her to get better and she could not live the rest of her life with it on. She reached up and undid the latch. "You're right, I'm just being silly." she said while pulling it off.

She felt exposed and uncomfortable especially with how all the adults, the worst of which were the doctors, were staring at her. Treegar stepped closer to the kids and crouched down. "Hi, I didn't introduce myself earlier. I'm Madison, I'm here to make sure that you and my sick friend here stay safe."

24

Days post Virus- 4-9

*   *   *

The house settled into something of a rhythm after that. All feelings of hurt over kept secrets were buried as the kids seemed to multiply and swarm, asking endless questions of all the adults regarding their journey and jobs. They seemed particularly interested in Treegar, though as far as Charissa had observed, the soldier never used more than a sentence or two to answer their barrage of questions.

Jason and Jaspreet were more loquacious but had been definitely relegated to third and fourth favorites. Penelope was always number one. Charissa felt that she had become a solid number five, only beating out the still unconscious Garner.

She still shared Penelope's big bed with the kids but other than that, they didn't seek her out. With most of the bodies out of the house and everyone knowing about each other, the kids finally had the run of the place. Without the constant threat of the infected banging on their walls, Sophia and Atticus were actually cheerful. They got up early and spent the whole day following the strangers around, poking their unconscious friend, and asking unending questions.

They watched the alien creatures with the same wonder they used to show when visiting the aquarium or zoo. These weren't scary beings that didn't belong on Earth, they were cool and different and getting rid of the scary things. Charissa tried explaining to them what she'd observed about the different types but they'd already heard most of that from either their mom or Jaspreet.

Once the creatures had cleared off their lawn and Charissa could no longer take the feeling of being a fifth wheel, she set a project for herself. She went to the basement and found a shovel, then she put on her gear and went outside. She didn't go far, just to the recently cleared front lawn, and started digging.

She cut through the first layer of grass and set the chunks aside. The ground underneath was heavy from the long winter. A couple hours of work and it began to rain again, turning the already heavy soil into a sloppy mess. After the third time more soil slopped off her shovel than she actually managed to throw out, Charissa called it a day.

"So, what was that?" Penelope asked from the top of the stairs. Her left hand was fisted and resting on her hip while her right side leaned against the wall.

"Tim needs a grave." Charissa admitted, "and I needed something to do."

Penelope nodded, not looking surprised at all. "Thank you." She glanced down the hall, "I hadn't gotten that far. I should have…"

Charissa cut that line of thought off, "And when exactly would you have done it? Today was the best opportunity we've had."

Penelope snorted, "You're right. Could haves and should haves don't help anything. I'll help you tomorrow though."

It was Charissa's turn to snort, "only if you can find a shovel. Took me a bit to find this one."

"Then we can take turns. It's about time you learned to share."

"Hey! I share plenty." She retorted, "but sharing is a good idea." she stretched her shoulders a bit, feeling the tightness that had gathered there, "I might have overdone it a little today."

"You poor dear." Penelope said dryly. "Luckily for you we still have hot water. Go take a bath before you sink up the house."

Charissa stifled a rather dark joke about how Timothy was already doing that job for her and began shucking off her gear instead.

*   *   *

It took three days to dig the hole. The last day was spent with one person at the bottom filling buckets with gravel and rocks and then handing them to the other person to dump out. They used a ladder against the wall of the hole to get out at the end of the day. In the end they had a hole deeper than Charissa was tall and larger than Timothy was by a fair amount.

The next day was a somber one. Penelope and Charissa wrapped Timothy in a sheet so the kids wouldn't see how his features had deformed over the past week. He had shifted from a generally green shade into something more red, as though the blood in his skin was oxidizing. He hardly looked like the man they had known.

Sophia and Atticus held hands and followed as their mother and aunt acted as pallbearers. Treegar, Jason, and Jaspreet trailed along behind, participating in the mourning of a man they had never known.

Charissa and Penelope crouched at the lip of the hole, lowering Timothy as far as their arms could reach. Charissa released his feet first, they hit the bottom of the grave with a wet thud. Penelope released one side of the sheet making his body twist. With as much care as she could she let the final corner slip. Timothy slipped more than fell into his grave.

All that needed to be said had already been expressed so this time they instead took turns covering him with dirt and rocks. It was a slow process and at the end the freshly turned soil mounded up. Charissa and Penelope had saved the largest rocks for last and began piling those atop the mound. Sophia and Atticus joined in, lifting the largest rocks they could and dropping them onto the pile.

Jason and the other's stood vigil, the soldier in particular spent most of the time watching their surroundings and making sure there was not a single hint of threat.

With Timothy finally buried and the family dirty and tired, they all retired to the house.

*　　*　　*

Charissa jerked awake, the echo of a gunshot ringing in her mind. It took her less than a second to be out of bed and skidding down the hall, the startled faces of her family flashing before her as she moved. Her body made it to the living room before her mind caught up with her actions.

Treegar was kneeling by the window aiming her rifle at something outside.

"Are we under attack?" She demanded, peering past the soldier and trying to see what was happening.

"No but the grave is." Treegar responded calmly, repositioning her gun and taking another shot.

Charissa finally got a good view out the open window and saw how the pile of rocks on Timothy's grave had been scattered, the soil ripped up in several spots. Several of the alien creatures were tearing into the bodies of their kinsmen while others advanced on the grave.

Treegar shot again, downing a Mid and sending its companions scattering for a moment before they reconverged on their now dead companion. That seemed to be her general strategy.

"You couldn't have warned someone?" Charissa asked

sarcastically, her heart thundering and her ears echoing. She told herself that she didn't mind Treegar, the woman seemed to be doing her best and was certainly battling her own fairly significant demons, but she definitely didn't like her.

"This seemed more urgent." Then the soldier tilted her head, "Oh, did I frighten the children?" That part was said with genuine regret.

"You did. I'll go tell them that you're defending their Dad's grave." Then under her breath, "And you'll be even more their hero."

"Hmm?" Treegar glanced away from the lawn, "I'm not a hero. I've been trying to tell them that. What I do... who I am... It's hard to explain. But what you did to protect them, I think you're the real hero. They just haven't seen what I've done so it's easier to romanticize."

That was the longest speech Charissa had heard from the woman and she wasn't sure how to respond. She settled for a simple nod and "okay," before turning and making her way back to the bedroom.

"What's wrong?" Penelope asked. Both children had huddled into her and she covered their heads with softly stroking hands.

"The creatures are trying to get to Timothy. Treegar is working on defending him. She apologizes for not warning us but wanted to act quickly to stop them." Charissa read a little between the lines of what Treegar had told her but was feeling slightly softer toward the woman than she had been a few minutes ago.

"Oh!" Atticus exclaimed, popping his head up from his mother's stomach.

"I wanna see!" Cried Sophia.

They both jumped up, scampering out of the room in a flash of gangly limbs, Atticus yelling "Me too! Me too!" behind his sister.

Charissa turned and thought about stopping them but it was already too late, they were out the door. "I don't think they should see that."

"Maybe not ordinarily, but after everything else? It might be nice for them to feel a sense of control over everything." Penelope observed, slipping out of the bed herself.

"Maybe, but what about the noise? Or after, how is seeing that going to affect their brain development?"

"If the past months have shown me anything, it is that we can't protect them from everything."

25

Days after Xeno-1- 10

*   *   *

Jason massaged Garner's legs and then checked his catheter. Thankfully Treegar and Jaspreet had accidentally grabbed the stuff for that during their hospital trip. When Garner had been dehydrated, worrying about him urinating hadn't been high on Jason's list of concerns, but now that he was getting proper fluids it was another story. The collection bag wasn't full so Jason left it, they didn't have so many of those that he was willing to waste one.

Dealing with a long term coma patient wasn't part of Jason's experience. Even during his residency he'd never dealt with one even on the short term and most of the care he was providing was something a nurse would be better trained to provide. It didn't help that he knew his patient and owed his life to him. It really didn't help that he felt all his care was useless and that Garner was already gone.

In fact, he felt like a lot of what he'd done was useless. With the way those creatures were seeking out Timothy's body he knew that Agatha's was long since eaten. Her pseudo grave in the snow wouldn't have lasted long and she had no one to defend her.

It was a heavy thought to process.

Treegar shot another creature and for a moment Jason wished he was the one firing. His anger was ridiculous and he knew it. When the things had been eating the infected, he was grateful to them, but when they wanted to eat someone he knew he got angry. He was so angry with them for probably eating his friend and frustrated with himself for the double standard. It hurt knowing that even that little bit of her was gone.

A rage churned in his stomach, heavy and hard. He hated them. He hated Xeno-1, he hated the creatures, and most of all he hated the beings that had sent them. In that moment Jason cursed God for allowing these calamities to happen.

Treegar fired again and Jason celebrated the death her bullet caused.

*   *   *

Garner wasn't doing well. It was a simple fact that the longer his coma lasted the worse his prognosis became. Jason performed the maintenance, Jaspreet and Treegar spelling him off as necessary. It wasn't onerous but it was consistent. Garner needed his bags changed, both fluids and urine. He needed his limbs moved and massaged to prevent atrophy and blood clots. He needed to be moved to prevent bed sores. It was a lot of work, Jason wasn't young or used to this kind of physical exertion.

Despite all that effort, Garner wasn't improving. The burn where his hand used to be was slowly healing, they'd managed to stave off infection in that area. But the burn on his leg hadn't been as lucky. Even with Xeno-1 no longer active, the injury had admitted a secondary infection.

Worst of all, they were running low on IV fluids and bandages. Jason knew that another raid of the hospital would need to be done if they were to continue Garner's care but before that he needed to discuss the reality of the situation with Treegar, and hope she didn't freak out on him.

While Jason prepared himself for that unpleasant conversation, he inventoried what they had left and wrote a wish list so they could be more targeted in their supply acquisition.

Treegar fired off three more shots and then took a break from guarding TImothy's grave to visit the washroom.

Jason looked out the window and briefly fingered Treegar's rifle, considering how it must feel to put a bullet into one of those creatures. He didn't act on the fantasy, Treegar would certainly be unhappy with him wasting one of their remaining bullets and he had no idea if he was even capable of hitting anything he aimed at.

The Mids and Littles fed just as easily on the Bigs and Mids that she had killed as they had on the infected. Apparently they had no moral or evolutionary objections to eating their own kind.

Treegar returned from the bathroom and frowned at his hand on her gun but didn't say anything. Jason snatched his hand away and watched her move through the living room. With her bare face and hands she looked frighteningly normal. She brushed her fingers across Garner's socked feet with a casual intimacy that made Jason deeply uncomfortable to witness considering the conversation he knew he needed to initiate.

"I can teach you." She said, nodding to her gun and then resuming her earlier position by the window.

"What? Oh! Jason stumbled over his thoughts for a moment. He would love to learn, if only to be able to fight back against the creatures pushing him out of his planet, but that wasn't why he was here. "Maybe some other time. I have something I need to talk to you about."

Treegar looked at him expectantly, she had this way of blanking her face as though whoever lived in there had stepped out for a moment.

"It's about Garner." Her face snapped back into animation, her brow furrowing and her lips tugging down. She remained silent but Jason could tell she was actively listening, waiting for him to finally continue.

"He hasn't improved." Jason licked his lips. He had rehearsed this in his mind a thousand times in a thousand different ways and none of those had been this stupid and stilted. "His leg, it isn't getting better. And you've noticed he hasn't woken up."

At that she nodded.

"Well, you see, he hasn't even had lucid moments. His body is functioning but it's like his mind isn't there. And, well, that's what I wanted to talk to you about. Part of it. You see..." He was bungling this and he knew it. He kept pausing and stumbling over his words like a stupid teenager asking a girl to the prom, or he guessed like it was his first time telling a scary woman with a gun that the man he was pretty sure she loved was essentially a vegetable.

"Xeno-1." He whispered, "It worked partly by damaging the minds of its hosts. Even though Garner wasn't infected for very long and the nature of his infection was clearly unusual, I am concerned that he has the same brain damage I've seen in other victims."

"Okay," Treegar breathed the word, her face having morphed back to its terrifying blankness, "what does that mean?"

Jason licked his lips, wishing he had a glass of water to moisten his parched mouth and throat. "He may never wake up. It means that his body," he waved over to the couch where Garner lay, propped on his side by several pillows, "may be all that's left of him."

"Are you suggesting?" Treegar let the question hang, though there was a coldness to her voice that reminded Jason of the winter winds at the beginning of their journey.

"No!" He gasped, wanting to pull back from this conversation completely, "but eventually, we will need to think about that. If the infection on his leg gets any worse, or if he develops heart or breathing problems. There might be nothing we can do. Even if we had a fully staffed hospital, we have no way of fixing what has happened to his brain. If he doesn't wake up on his own, we can't do anything more than we are already doing." He paused before forging on to his second task.

"Also, we are running low on supplies again. We have enough to continue his care for another two days but then we will be back to dressing his wounds with whatever Penelope and Charissa have on hand and giving him fluids orally."

Treegar nodded slowly, "I can handle that." She looked outside and froze. It was worse than her blank face and sent every fiber in Jason screaming that something was wrong.

He followed her line of sight. Descending from the gray clouds was an oblong tan... vessel? As more of it dropped below the clouds Jason began to get a sense of scale. The thing was massive. It looked like a container ship descending on them.

It grew in size until the shadow it cast had completely blotted out the sun, sending the house into a false twilight. The closer it got the more certain he became that it was going to land on them and crush them.

26

Landing day

*   *   *

Madison's monkey brain screamed at her to run but her legs remained locked into stunned immobility. As the bottom of it hit far off roofs light began to crest the top, bringing daylight back. The sound of buckling houses tore through the otherwise silent air.

While the ship was setting down, Penelope, Charissa, Dr. Nagi, and the children came out to see what was causing the noise. Treegar allowed their reactions to slide over her, too consumed in her own horror to pay them real attention.

Behind the desire to flee rose a secondary emotion, a bone shaking rage at everything before her. The monsters in that vessel, and she knew in her gut that was what they were, were responsible for everything. They had sent a virus designed to weaken and destroy. Then, unwilling to see the results of their terrible creation, they sent a clean up crew. Now they were going to move in and take up residence on the homes of those they had murdered. They had broken her mind and stolen Garner's and now, now they were here to steal their planet.

The callous greed of their actions spoke for them. She didn't care how fancy their ship was, what technological marvels they might have wrought, or that they were an advanced alien species. She wanted them dead. She wanted it to be as though they had never existed.

She picked up her gun and with careful, cold calculation counted her bullets. A small hand gripped her side and she spared a glance for the little boy who now clung to her. Atticus looked at her with an existential fear that no child his age should experience.

The rest of the group gasped and she looked back up to see a seam had formed at the closest end of the vessel. It widened and a ramp began to stretch out in a gentle slope, extending until it touched the ground most of the way across the street and only a house length down. The ramp crushed the houses it went through without a single moment of pause.

What she could see of the interior of the ship was a lighter shade of the same tan with a soft yellow light. Figures gathered at the top of the ramp and began making their way down it. They were beige, bipedal and had a long triangular tail sliding behind them. The closer they got the more they began to resemble kangaroos. But the light glinted off their hides as though it was composed of a hard polished substance rather than fur. Large dish shaped ears swiveled on their head and a collection of black dots comprised what Treegar assumed were their eyes.

Atticus pulled on her a little harder. Treegar looked down at him, glancing back at the approaching aliens and then crouched to be at his eye level. "I'm going to go protect us." He met her gaze and then nodded, releasing his grip on her and stepping back.

"I'm coming." Dr. Scordato announced.

Treegar just nodded, "Take Garner's gun." What she wouldn't give to have Garner at her side during this fight instead of the doctor, but no, without Garner there she could do whatever it took to stop this. No holding back.

"Me too," Said Charissa, "I've got my own gun." She rushed out of the room and down the hall.

Treegar stood up, "Everyone else, get back and stay safe." She met Penelope's eyes and the Jaspreets. Both women nodded and began herding the children away from the living room and down the hall. They passed Charissa on her way back out.

"We do this fast and we don't give them a chance to respond," Treegar ordered. "The two of you go out the front door, I'll start here and pick them off. Both of you run and get on that ship before they close the door. Kill them like they tried to kill us."

When they both turned away Madison took a moment to look at Garner's sleep softened face before taking her position at the window.

Five aliens had made it to the bottom of the ramp. They were waving something around and gesturing to each other. They seemed to be looking for something and possibly arguing. Treegar noted that the alien creatures had scattered, like prey recognizing their natural predator. She picked out a target and readied her weapon.

They had reached the lawn of the house so she could make out specific details. Her target was the tallest of the group, their skin a shimmering golden hue made up almost entirely of interlocking scales, tiny ones on its face and large almost fist sized ones around its back and down the tail. They all made chittering noises intermingled with selections of lower tones and guttural punctuations. Sounds which Treegar knew her throat wasn't designed to imitate.

She aimed for the aliens' beady eyes and fired. It jerked back and dropped. She didn't give its companions a chance to react, selecting a second target and shooting it within a heartbeat of its companion. By then Scordato and Charissa had opened the door. The three remaining aliens turned and fled toward the ship in great bounds. Treegar missed her third shot as she hadn't anticipated the distance the aliens could cover in a single leap, but managed to account for their strange movements with her fourth.

Scordato and Charissa raced after the aliens, reaching the edge of the ramp in seconds. Treegar squeezed out another shot, hitting the fourth alien and sending it flying off the ramp and into the ruins of one of the houses they had landed on.

The fifth alien made it inside the ship but Treegar watched as Charissa paused and raised her own gun. The alien fell, Charissa's bullet having found its mark.

Treegar raced away from the window, barreling out the front door and sprinting across the road and up the ramp. Scordato and Charissa had a head start in the assault on the alien vessel. Treegar passed two more alien bodies, each with shots to their main body as well as their heads, before she caught up with the others.

They were firing down a long corridor at the retreating backs of three aliens. She saved her bullets, choosing instead to simply run after their prey. Scordato and Charissa quickly followed her lead. The corridor turned a corner and Treegar slowed just before it, peaking around to assess the danger. There was none. The aliens had taken refuge behind a door and left no obvious defenses behind them.

Treegar approached the door and touched what looked like a handle. When it didn't budge she shot it. Her bullet tore through whatever metal it was made of and made the door shudder. She dug her fingers into the hole and reefed on the door until it slid open. Beyond it two aliens stood waiting for them.

They leaned back on their tails and let out a guttural roar, kicking out at Treegar. She threw herself to the side, one of the kicks grazing her ribs and sending her off course to smash into the wall. Charissa and Scordato fired their guns, bullets tearing into the aliens and making them drop twitching to the floor.

A second round was fired into each of their heads, sending gray fluid spattering the corridor and pooling on the floor.

Treegar shoved herself up, a searing pain emanating from where the aliens had kicked her. "Don't let them kick you." She grunted to her companions and then limped down the next segment of the corridor.

They had to waste bullets along the way, forcing doors open into empty sections. Eventually they shot open a door and found more aliens. The space beyond the door had been piled up with a variety of strange objects forming a barricade against the oncoming humans.

The three of them pushed the objects away, many of the smaller items shifting with little effort. The variety of objects and the haphazard manner they had been thrown against the door was ridiculous. Treegar was honestly surprised because all of the corridors they had gone through hadn't had half this much stuff in them combined. The voices beyond the barricade chittered and moaned, occasionally throwing some of the fallen objects back at the attacking humans.

Treegar got a clear view of one of the aliens and fired, sending the creature backward and out of her line of sight. The other aliens increased their cries and moans in both pitch and volume. Her ears hurt both from firing her gun in an enclosed space and the added frequencies of the alien screams.

More of the barricade fell away, another large object destabilizing and falling into the room. It took several surrounding items with it and opened the view into the room considerably. Treegar ducked to avoid a small object flung at her head and then opened fire. She could see four large aliens standing between her and several slightly smaller aliens. She had already shot two before their positions took on any meaning to her. Her third shot catching one of the smaller aliens as realization hit her.

She paused in her shooting, though Scordato and Charissa continued.

This was a nursery.

She felt sick. They were killing children. Parents and children.

Her earlier rage was extinguished by what they were doing. Bullets tore through the remaining adults and juveniles. Gray blood sprayed across the room and across the faces of the smallest children.

These aliens hadn't put up any kind of actual defense. Their only actions had been to defend their young. It was so basic and relatable that Treegar felt her stomach surge and reject her own actions.

She turned her head and threw up. The yellow brown of her vomit blended with the tan of the floor.

"Were those?" Charissa's voice contained the same horror and fear that Treegar felt in her gut.

"I think they were," Scordato confirmed, his own voice barely registering above a whisper.

Treegar stared at what they had just done. Knowing that it was self defense, that she was protecting human children, even hating the adults for what they had done to Earth, didn't lessen the revulsion she felt at killing them and their young. Her hearing slowly cleared from all the gunshots, though the fearful chittering continued to echo inside her skull.

A screech ripped through the air. Treegar watched in horror as the chest of one of the adults undulated. She raised her gun, horror overwhelming guilt. A tiny paw clawed its way out followed by another and then a head with long ears flopped over its eyes. The critter shook its head, the ears shifting to settle at the side of its head. Tiny hooked claws found catches on the large scales and the baby used them to crawl fully out of the pouch and along its parents body.

Treegar lowered her gun as the baby dipped out of view, her heart breaking as the sounds it made suddenly shifted into a soft keening.

"We should…" Scordato gestured to the pile of dead parents.

Treegar shook her head, she couldn't. Though she knew that her job was to do these hard things, this was a step too far. She had already done damage that she knew Garner would disapprove of but that could be excused by fear and ignorance, this would be cold blooded murder of the innocent.

"I can't." Charissa murmured.

Scordato nodded, looking out of the room, "We should look for others."

Treegar nodded and turned away from the evidence of their crimes.

27

Charissa felt ill. She couldn't determine if it was a reaction to what they'd done or if it was her body coming down from an adrenaline high. As they made their way down the corridor, double checking all the rooms they had broken into earlier, she considered their situation. She felt justified in attacking the aliens. They had tried to destroy all life on Earth and then replace it with their own. It was narrow minded and horrible. Their approach spoke to an inability, or lack of desire, to see value in what Earth already had to offer.

Xeno-1 had been so heavy handed it was like using a wrecking ball where a scalpel would have been efficient. Logically, she could understand getting rid of humans; they were messy, destructive, and not at all prone to sharing with strangers. But Xeno-1 had been designed to kill so broadly that birds and every mammal it encountered had been destroyed. It had ruined delicate ecosystems and slapping a different species in their place wasn't going to fix it.

The creatures they sent to clean up after Xeno-1 showed a callous desire to ignore the realities of what they had done. To make it so that the only confrontation they'd have with their crimes would be the buildings and monuments that remained. Charissa wondered if Earth was their first planet to destroy like this or if they'd done this to countless other worlds, eliminating billions of unique creatures and then supplanting them. After a moment's consideration she knew that that was just what they'd done. If Earth had been their first they wouldn't have been so brazen and self assured as to land and begin their colonization without assuring themselves that all life had already been eradicated. They might have at least been armed to deal with possible resistance. But they'd come out unarmed and had shown a genuine shock and fear when Treegar had begun to shoot them. Besides, a race that would die to defend their young wouldn't also bring those young onto an unconquered planet, would they?

Honestly, with the brutality of Xeno-1 she would have expected the Aliens to tear through Treegar, Jason, and herself. But they'd barely fought back, displaying nothing that resembled a weapon more than an improvised projectile.

Charissa followed along blindly as Treegar and Jason led the way through the maze of the ship. Most of the rooms held pods and crates. They didn't dig further into their contents, focusing solely on finding surviving adults. She honestly didn't know if she would be able to kill them if they did find any. Her anger had drained away and only an empty shell remained.

It took them a long time to feel like they had searched the ship, but beyond the bodies of those they had already killed they saw no other aliens.

"What should we do?" Charissa asked her companions.

"I'm going back for the babies." Treegar stated, her voice oddly flat in a way that terrified Charissa.

"You can't!" She gasped, the woman was cold but even she couldn't kill a baby, could she?

"They'll die on their own. I'll accept the responsibility." Treegar didn't wait for a reply to her shocking statement.

Charissa gaped as the soldier she had thought so badly of made the choice to accept and protect an alien baby, the child of Earth's invaders. It took her only a moment to rush after Treegar.

"What are you doing?" Jason called after both of them.

Charissa turned and jogged backwards for a moment while replying, "I'm going with her. There's probably more than the one we saw and she'll need help. Go check on Penelope and the kids and let them know what's happened, okay?"

*   *   *

There were four surviving babies. As they'd pushed through the carnage, gray blood spreading on their hands, they'd discovered the bodies of several more that had been shot along with their parents or crushed when those parents fell. The survivors didn't seem to know they should fear Charissa and Treegar, climbing right into the women's arms and hiding inside their jackets. They ranged in size from the largest who was about the size of a toddler to the smallest which Charissa could almost fit in her coat pocket. That one had still been in its parents pouch and was only found due to its wrigglings and squeaks.

She wasn't sure how they were going to keep them alive. What did alien babies eat? What kind of care would they need? The list of what she didn't know about them felt endless. Presumably their parents would have known what they needed but because of Charissa, Treegar, and Jason they weren't here anymore. Although if their parents had had their way then Charissa, Treegar, Jason, Penelope, Sophia, Atticus, and what remained of earth life wouldn't exist anymore, so in balance, despite her guilt, she knew their actions had been justified.

For lack of knowing what else to do, they brought the babies back to the house with them.

*   *   *

It didn't take more than a few minutes for Sophia and Atticus to decide that the babies were the cutest things they'd ever seen. After some initial questions with regards to where they came from and what they were, they settled into cuddling and playing with the little critters. The largest one was the most active, hopping around and poking at everything. The littlest slept, at least that was what Charissa assumed it was doing, most of the time.

With the children enjoying the babies, Charissa opened the discussion about how they were going to care for the babies. "Eventually they are going to get hungry and I have no idea what they eat."

"Well," Treegar began, her voice softer than usual, "we should start with what is in the containers. Presumably they had food with them on board. If we find something that looks like it might be food we can offer it to them and see what happens."

"Your solution is to experiment on them?" Charissa was horrified but could also see the logic in the suggestion.

"All parenting is experimental. I don't see an alternative."

Jason chimed in, "And feeding them our food could be worse. Considering what the chatter online says has happened to people who have eaten the creatures they sent, I imagine that our food would be just as incompatible to them."

Charissa looked at him blankly and then shuddered, "People have actually been eating those things?"

He huffed, "They've tried. Desperate people are willing to try just about anything. Do none of you keep up on what's going on out there?"

Everyone except Jaspreet shook their heads, she just shrugged and said, "I look at different sites than you."

Charissa had stopped spending as much time online in the past weeks, ever since Ryosuke and his group had attacked she hadn't felt safe even with that limited amount of contact. The added stress of having strangers, who she really needed to stop thinking of as such, in the house had left her too occupied to worry about the wider world in anything other than the vaguest of ways.

"Right, so basically, our bodies can't process whatever they are made of. It is essentially poison to us. It would probably be the same with our food for them although without a better understanding of what they do eat we can't be sure of that. It is better to stick to feeding them only stuff from their ship for now."

"Okay, that's fair." Charissa agreed, though now she was thinking about the potential problems they were going to face with a planet overrun with creatures that humans couldn't eat and a dearth of creatures they could eat.

They stood in silence, watching the lively and sweet interactions between Sophia, Atticus, and the baby aliens.

"Why did they land here?" Penelope asked, looking away from her kids and peering through the living room windows at the mammoth silhouette of the alien vessel.

"They looked like they were looking for something." Treegar supplied.

"Oh!" Jaspreet gasped.

Everyone turned to watch as a flash of insight lit up the scientist's face.

"The meteorite!" She turned to Jason, "They must have a way of detecting the metal from the meteorite. There is no other explanation for why they would land precisely here. They must have come to collect it." She huffed, "it must have been pretty confusing for their sensors when it wasn't in one piece like they sent it." She pursed her lips and scowled, gesturing to the mostly reconstructed meteorite sitting in a corner of the living room.

Charissa looked between the pearlescent sheen of the lattice, the playing alien babies, and the alien ship. So much had changed in the past few months, all due to the whims and ramifications of these three things. She watched her niece and nephew playing with the offspring of beings who had actively planned their death, who were obliquely responsible for the deaths of their father and great aunt. Her heart ached and she had to wonder if there would come a day where Sophia would look at their companions and see them as murderers or if the blind forgiveness they gave them now would last.

EPILOGUE

Greg kicked his feet up and leaned back in his chair. This was the first break he'd given himself in the last three days and he was going to enjoy it.

Three days since the alien colony ships, because that's what they had determined they most likely were, had landed on Earth. They had landed at nearly the same time though astronomers and alien enthusiasts were working out how the variance in landing times might be used to determine the direction of origin of the ships. Greg had confirmation that most of the ships had been attacked and over powered shortly after landing. Greg couldn't blame the people who had done the attacking, after months of lockdowns and zombies and alien corpse eaters the chance to finally strike back at those who had caused so much suffering must have been overwhelming. Thinking about it made Greg wish that he'd had the opportunity to do some striking back of his own.

A few had been attacked before they'd opened. Those had responded much more passively than Greg would have expected, picking up and leaving Earth's atmosphere rather than shooting their attackers. This passive reaction fit with the reports Greg had received of how the Aliens behaved on an individual level. In nearly every one of the confrontations with the aliens, they had presented only minimal resistance, choosing to flee and barricade themselves away rather than fight back.

Satellite tracking of the vessels showed them in a very high orbit of Earth, remaining a constant threat despite their retreat. That threat had led to surviving governments, mostly in Europe,

Africa, and Australasia, drafting a coalition pact agreeing to aid each other in repelling further alien incursions. Greg and what remained of the Canadian government had agreed, though with their current circumstances honoring it in more than just name would be nearly impossible.

In fact, they were lucky that the alien vessels chose to land in the more habitable longitudes of Earth's surface, if they'd chosen to land much further north there was a good chance that no one would be around to repel them as Canada's great white north had been the hardest hit by Xeno-1.

The most pressing question was where humanity might go from here. North America had been stripped of animal life and most of its people. Entire ecosystems were overturned. With the coming spring trees, plants, and insects that depended on the local fauna would be affected. The remaining human population would be forced into veganism by the simple lack of animal protein.

Greg pushed those concerns away and closed his eyes. He would think about that later, for now he had earned a rest.

*   *   *

Jason poked his way through the screens. Though the panel was smooth like glass it contained divots and bumps some of which he needed a tool to press the bottom of. The screen displayed text and images in a variety of shades of brown. That was something he'd discovered while exploring the ship, everything was in either brown or yellow. The next most common color was gray with a rust red coming in a distant fourth. No blues, no greens and no true black. He wondered what that meant about their eyesight. Or, maybe there was a cultural prohibition against cooler colors?

He had no idea what their lettering said but he was carefully documenting each screen and the button press which got him to it. Every night he uploaded more of his findings to his colleagues online and let them pick it over. There was speculation regarding some symbols and their possible meaning though the linguists insisted that they needed more context before translation could even be hazarded. Until then, Jason was just glad to be doing something useful again. This felt more like research and less like the groping in the dark of the past several months.

He might have been instrumental in stopping Xeno-1, but he wasn't certain his actions had actually done anything other than endanger those around him. It was the aliens, the "Roos" as people had taken to calling them, that had actually turned off their virus. He'd just been there. It was disheartening to know that in these squiggles and lines lay more knowledge of microscopic pathogens than Jason had learned in a lifetime of study.

Jaspreet had lucked out yesterday by finding what she concluded must be star charts. Today she was voraciously devouring them, taking pictures and even video of the screen in front of her.

It was strange, despite knowing that the aliens were still out there, circling the Earth, and despite knowing that the remaining militaries were mobilizing to confront or repel those aliens, Jason felt as though he could finally relax. Those were someone else's problems. All he could do for now was help other experts translate an alien language by taking and uploading pictures.

*　　*　　*

Charissa watched as Treegar fed George from a bottle. They'd found crates of substances that seemed to equate to formula, at least once it was mixed with sterile water it made a substance that the babies seem to like. They'd named the babies just to make it easier when talking about them. They were in order of size: Paul, Jamie, Taylor, and George.

While Paul and Jamie were pretty active and seemed smart they couldn't mimic human sounds. When the humans tried mimicking their sounds they just made the babies confused, though George seemed to think it was a silly game and would make increasingly difficult noises for them to copy. What had been working was a combination of gestures and sign language.

If Charissa or someone else taught them a gesture and showed them an object then repeated the gesture they seemed to associate the gesture with the object. They were up to at least fifty words and Charissa was starting to have a hard time remembering some of the less used gestures.

The hardest part was not knowing if what they were doing was right. She'd ventured online a few days ago to see if there was anyone else out there who could help and had met with a barrage of people calling for the extermination of alien life, on Earth and elsewhere. It made sense. They were angry and scared. The aliens had attacked them. Despite that, Charissa couldn't contemplate killing these babies. It had only been a few days but whether from guilt or misplaced maternal feelings, she loved them.

She'd left that space fairly quickly and asked Jaspreet and Jason not to share the baby's existence with their colleagues. She had no idea how long keeping them hidden would protect them but she wanted to keep the proverbial target off their backs for as long as possible. Maybe if they learned to communicate, those people calling for their deaths would be able to see them as something separate from their parents. It was a long shot but it was something that she clung to.

*   *   *

Madison used one hand to sign, "Ball, throw, jump," to Jamie. The child bounced with excitement and brought her the ball. In the moment between signing and Jamie returning with the ball, she shifted her hold on George so she could more easily support the infant and the bottle they were attached to. It had been really lucky that Penelope still had a few of Atticus's old bottles in the basement and even more lucky that the nipple shape was similar enough to whatever the Roo parents fed their babies with that George and the others hadn't objected to their use.

Jamie dropped the ball in front of her and she bent down to scoop it up, beginning the simple game they had devised. She threw the ball above Jamie's head and he jumped to an astounding height to try and grab it. He missed, which he did about fifty percent of the time, and he hopped after the ball and then brought it back to Madison, dropping it and then signing, "More, more."

Jamie could play this game for hours and had over the past two days. Her days were pretty well filled between the babies and caring for Garner. The animals that had been trying to dig up Timothy's grave seemed permanently scared off by the ship and the Roo babies so she'd been able to abandon her vigil and free up Dr. Scordato from that particular duty.

Sophia and Atticus delighted in playing games with the larger babies and cuddling the smaller ones. The shadows that had been over them the entire time Madison and Treegar had known them were dissipating though she knew they were not yet, and may never be, wholly gone. Penelope had expressed how grateful she was that the past year hadn't taken away their sense of wonder and compassion. Madison hoped that that would stand true for the rest of humanity as well.

After Dr. Scordato's comment, she had ventured online, updating her social media accounts to let those who might care know that she was alive and reading over the top news articles. People were terrible and they were showing it in the clamor they were making on the internet. Treegar watched the babies and prepared herself for what she might have to do if any of those voices ventured out of cyberspace and into the real world.

She'd gone on a supply run to the hospital the day after the aliens landed, taking only Jaspreet and filling the SUV with everything on Jason's list. They did three trips that day, luckily not seeing any other humans. They had boxes of gauze and fluid, enough to last Garner a good while. She hoped it was enough to last until he woke up.

Jamie hopped back to her and gave her the ball, hopping about halfway across the room and then eagerly watching her and waiting for her to throw. She made a show of winding up and then let the ball soar through the air, nearly hitting the ceiling. Jamie jumped and caught the ball, wrapping his body around it and forming his own ball.

Madison cheered and Jamie let out a matching trill of triumph.

The End

www.ingramcontent.com/pod-product-compliance
Lightning Source LLC
Chambersburg PA
CBHW051447050726
47593CB00005B/1960